When Eunice Saint Jacques meets Adrien Ascott at the Halloween party of one of New Orleans's prestigious hotels, she thinks he's cute. Nah, she thinks he's the most gorgeous creature ever. Little does she know he isn't all that he seems to be, and that this Halloween will seal her destiny forever.

While it's Presentation Night at Club Sortilege, the renowned New Orleans BDSM club, Yvette Carlisle, the Grand Master's slave, is worried. What happened to her friend Eunice should never have happened.

Not now.

Hell, not for a long time.

Yet, here she is, talking to Adrien and uncovering an age-old curse that dates back to 1890 and makes his karma as deadly as that of Count Dracula himself. Is it true, or is he spinning just another tale of bondage and sadism in the plush lounge of Club Sortilege?

Deadly Karma
Copyright © 2020 Laura Tolomei
ISBN: 978-1-4874-3160-0
Cover art by Angela Waters

Published by eXtasy Books Inc or
Devine Destinies, an imprint of eXtasy Books Inc

Look for us online at:
www.eXtasybooks.com or www.devinedestinies.com

DEADLY KARMA
A CLUB SORTILEGE TALE 1

BY

LAURA TOLOMEI

DEDICATION

To my friend and colleague, Guido Tavoletti, because your essence is still among us.

CHAPTER ONE: EUNICE

When Eunice met him, she thought he was cute.

Nah, whom was she kidding?

She thought he was the most gorgeous and perfect man in the world, but then she hadn't met too many men, which could explain why she was as bewitched as a schoolgirl.

Which she wasn't.

She was a full-grown woman with a job, friends, and all that jazz. The job was no more than a boring accountant's task at an international shipping agency. The friends were two at most, Yvette Carlisle and Palomar Redondo, but who needed more?

Eunice Saint Jacques had never been a popular girl. Despite her fancy last name and illustrious heritage dating back to a once noble and wealthy French family, she'd been the wallflower of every high school party. The one other girls giggled about behind her back, the one no one bothered to speak to, not even to say hi. During those formative years as the only child of Javier and Francine, she'd been pretty much on her own, the lonely student of Crestwood High School in St. Martinville, Louisiana.

That's where she'd been born and raised in utter misery and depression.

"Eunice, you stop that *immediately!*" Yvette's shrill voice startled her. "You hear?"

"Stop what?" Playing the innocent, she gazed at her friend's image in the mirror while studiously avoiding the reflection of herself.

"You know what." On the opposite side of Yvette, Palomar sounded exasperated. "That daydreaming stuff you're always so fond of."

"Moi?" Eunice's attempt at a joke failed to move either of her friends.

The three of them were crowded in her tiny–very tiny–flat in New Orleans. This desolate place was the refuge she'd managed to buy after ten-years' worth of savings, so minuscule that there was scarcely enough space for the three of them. It had the bare minimum, a microscopic kitchen, a convertible sofa that became her bed at nights, a disproportionally large closet, an acceptable bathroom, and a TV set. Unfortunately, also a mirror, the same one they were all squashed against and that would determine her fate tonight.

"Come off it, Eunice," Yvette's voice was gentler. "Stop fooling around and concentrate on the dress. What do you think?"

"Yeah, do try to make a serious contribution here," Palomar chimed in, less cranky as well. "Or it'll just be Yve and me busting our ass off to make you look nice."

"What's the point?" Reluctantly, Eunice returned her focus on her mirror image.

She wasn't precisely Miss America, so no way a dress could hide that simple fact, no matter how incredible it was. She was just too short and fat for anything to make her look thinner, if only for a night. Her constant dieting hadn't helped disintegrate the extra inches in her thighs and belly or the lumps she perceived on her hips. Her round, brown eyes and limp brown hair didn't improve her looks any, maybe because her face leaned toward the pudgy.

"I don't think it'll make any difference."

She was hopeless, after all, had been all her life, so why would things change any tonight?

"Of course, it will." Yvette stared at her with an optimism

Eunice was far from feeling. "Tonight's Halloween, and we've been invited to a very exclusive party in a very exclusive hotel."

"Yeah, I can't wait to get into La Maison del Fuego," Palomar squealed enthusiastically. "I've always wanted to go to their renown Halloween event but never dated anyone with the right connections."

"Now, we'll all get to go thanks to this fabulous Halloween party." Yvette giggled, twisting the fake whiskers that were part of her cat outfit.

Eunice watched her with a certain degree of envy. Yvette was everything she wasn't. Six feet tall, graceful, long, golden auburn hair and feline green eyes, with the miles-long legs of a runner, and a quick intelligence Eunice had come to respect over the three years she'd known her.

"I know it'll be great fun." Palomar's black eyes sparkled at the prospect.

She was another incredibly beautiful woman who bore her Creole ancestry with gracefulness and ease. Not too hard to do when you were five feet nine, had mysterious black eyes, luscious olive skin, regular features, and a mass of glossy black hair tumbling all over the place. Plus, her maid costume with the outrageously skimpy skirt, red stiletto heels, black fishnet stockings, and purplish feather duster strapped to her waist made Palomar look so sexy Eunice had no doubt men would be all over her. Vice versa, they wouldn't waste a single peek on her, Eunice Saint Jacques, dressed as Queen Elizabeth, the first, not the second.

"For you, I'm sure." Sadly, Eunice shook her head. "You look gorgeous in your costumes while I . . . ." Wrapped inside the most cumbersome outfit of all, she gazed one more time at her mirror image. "I look more like Henry the Eighth than his daughter Elizabeth."

True enough. What glared back at Eunice could've easily

passed for the lost original of Hans Holbein's famous painting rather than any of William Gaunt's renditions of the female sovereign.

"Nonsense!" Yvette dismissed her objection with a wave of a hand. "You look stately and regal, which is what Elizabeth was."

Yeah, anything but sexy. Eunice didn't share this observation because Yvette and Palomar would've reprimanded her for it. Eunice loved them for their fiercely protective attitude and sincere friendship. They had been her anchor and the reason she'd held onto a non-descript job as much as she had.

That was where they'd met, the three of them, Yvette and Palomar being the secretaries of the General Manager and the Chief of Operations of the renowned Goldblum Freight Services. They had proved to be invaluable for Eunice's peace of mind, but they simply couldn't get past some things.

Like the fact they were perfect while Eunice wasn't. Like the fact they had plenty of choices when it came to men while Eunice didn't. That none of them had a steady boyfriend wasn't relevant to Eunice's claim that she was a failure while Yvette and Palomar were successes.

"You'll find your prince handsome tonight." Palomar oozed confidence from every pore as she gave Eunice's wig the finishing touches.

"Queen Elizabeth was known as the Virgin Queen," Eunice quipped, feeling the weight of the wig on her forehead.

"All the more reason for Prince Charming to show up tonight." Yvette smiled, unmoved in her certainties. "You know how much they like virgins." She giggled.

If only Eunice could believe her.

"Technically, I'm not a virgin."

Not a hussy, either, if she had to admit. Her sex life was limited to half an hour in the school's parking lot and a couple of one-night stands. Not one of these experiences had been all that exciting, but then none of those men had exactly been too keen on her needs. More on theirs, their cocks demanding all her attention and giving little back except for a sore pussy and mouth. What they had in common was their quickness in going about it. Raising her legs, they had slammed into her without the slightest concern whether she was ready or not. Then, they had come in the blink of an eye while she was still wondering what she was feeling.

"Maybe, I should stay at home." Dubious, Eunice tried, not for the first time, to wriggle free from the invitation Yvette had sprung on her at the end of the working day.

"Oh, stop moping, and let's go." Palomar yanked her away from the mirror. "It's Halloween. You look good enough to eat, and La Maison del Fuego is waiting for us."

And that was the end of that.

CHAPTER TWO

"Here we are." Stepping out of the cab, Yvette looked around in evident satisfaction.

La Maison del Fuego was a superb hotel located in the French Quarter. The Halloween season brought out its best, decked out as it was with filthy-looking cobwebs and menacing devils peeping from every spotlight. A tall, ugly demon — probably Pan judging from its hoofs, tail, and flute — greeted guests in the foyer. More hellish creatures decorated the walls and the hallways leading to the main party chamber while hanging bats and spiders overhead frightened everyone.

"Wow!" Glancing up and around, Palomar sounded ecstatic. "This looks fantastic! Better than anything I've ever seen on Halloween."

Small wonder. La Maison del Fuego had a history of hosting the best Halloween events of all of New Orleans. Probably of all the world, though Eunice wouldn't know. She hadn't too much of an experience with fancy affairs, having been only to a couple of them since moving here from St. Martinville.

"Yeah, they outdid themselves." Yvette's enthusiasm was palpable. "Look at how creepy that is." She pointed to something on the ceiling.

Eunice looked and shivered. On the top right corner, there seemed to be a snake's den, judging from the many long, limbless reptiles running away from it. What scared her was the giant tarantula at the center of the vipers' nest, holding a couple of snakes down with hairy legs the size of baseball bats. The colossal spider was so massive it justified the snakes' panic. Eunice felt sorry for the two unfortunate victims it had already caught, both writhing in agony.

"Oh, gross," she croaked, flipping her gaze to something less horrific.

"I think it's awesome." Evidently unaffected, Palomar stared at the scene in rapt fascination. "Nothing like good old spiders and snakes to get you in the Halloween mood."

"That's why they're such masters here." Yvette nodded happily.

"Speaking of masters, shouldn't we show our invitations to someone?" Lucky for Eunice, her gaze had fallen on a stunning bouncer leaning on the frame of a door she guessed to be the main chamber. "Like to that guy over there?" She indicated for the girls' benefit.

"Now, that's what I call my kind of Superman." As her face split in a wide smile, Yvette studied the man with such an appreciative stare Eunice had to look at him again. A low table in front of him did not hide the man's body-builder frame. Even if he was stock still, his muscles rippled under that Superman outfit that had so impressed Yvette. No wonder she was drooling as she advanced toward him, invitations in hand.

Straightening, the man grinned at Yvette. "Can I help you, furry friend?"

"You most certainly can," Yvette purred deliciously. "I've always wanted to fly up in the sky in the arms of a hunk."

"Sorry." He picked up a pair of glasses and wore them. "I'm just Clark Kent at the moment."

"That's a real shame." Yvette's fingertips trailed on the man's beefy upper arm. "Why don't you give me a call when dear old Clark becomes Superman?"

The man's blatant appraisal of Yvette's seductive feline body was not lost on Eunice spying from a distance. "I'm sure he could spare a minute or two on Cat Woman if he isn't too busy." He licked his lips in palpable anticipation. "If she proves she isn't here to crash the party."

"Hey, we got invited to this joint." Yvette waved the thin red cards engraved in gold in front of the man's face before slamming them down on the table.

"I never doubted it." He bent his head in mock assurance. "Please, go right in." He picked up the cards and stuffed them inside a drawer.

"Remember, I'll be waiting for Superman." Without a second glance, Yvette swept past him, followed by Palomar and her loud clicking of stiletto heels on the marble floor.

Eunice couldn't breeze by nonchalantly. Her enormous Queen Elizabeth outfit got stuck between the table and the door. Only a good deal of push and shove managed to get her past Superman's sneering gaze, even if he did try to help by thrusting the table aside.

Humiliated, she hurried through and stopped after a few feet to get her bearings amidst the people, the loud music, and the candlelight.

Yeah, candlelight, can you believe it?

She couldn't.

Well, on closer inspection, she realized it wasn't candlelight at all. It was a modern-day electric fixture resembling a candle, but with the regrettable side effect that the light was no better. She was barely able to see.

When her eyes adjusted to the dimness, she spotted a counter at the far end where drinks were served. More Supermen hovered behind it, handing tall, frosted glasses to the long line of thirsty patrons. Making out a long cat's tail and a purplish duster, she moved to intercept.

"Ah, here you are, babe." Hooking a hand around her arm, Yvette dragged her forward. "What would you like to drink?"

Uncertain, Eunice glanced first at Palomar, then at Yvette.

"What are you gals having?"

Parties and drinks were still a new thing for her. If she knew them at all, it was thanks to the two women. They had coaxed her out of her shell. Just three years ago, Eunice had been pretty much a recluse, venturing outside only to go to work and get back home. That had been the extent of her outings if discounting a few nights at a singles' bar that had led to some unrepeatable sexual encounters. Since they had been far from satisfying, she would've gladly continued on her monotonous routine and forgotten there existed a life beyond a job, had not the agency hired two striking secretaries one after the other.

Yvette had been the first. She'd been assigned to Goldblum's GM, Tony Spencer, an ambitious man who thrived on an aesthetic sense and keen eye, meaning that he surrounded himself only with beautiful people, in and out of work. Of course, Yvette was a perfect fit, in and out of work. The fact Tony Spencer was a married man never stopped him from getting what he wanted.

Yvette had played along because he was such a great lay, Yvette's words, not Eunice's. Besides, she didn't like to be tied down, so fooling with a married man was what she'd been seeking all along. The fact he was her boss was only an extra incentive. On the side, Eunice knew she cultivated other bedmates, attractive men she used whenever Tony was unavailable, none of whom meant much of anything except fun under the sheets. Most shocking of all, Yvette had confessed to being a BDSM slave who played the field. Imagine that!

Eunice had enough problems figuring out what Yvette's enslavement was all about without delving into the etiquette of this unconventional lifestyle or the finer points of what was expected from each role. Her friend was happy with her choices, and that was all that mattered to Eunice.

Then, Goldblum had hired Palomar as Mike Walgate's

secretary. The last one quit on the spot after the ultimate clash with the Chief of Operations. Everybody knew Mike had a temper, and his secretaries often paid for it until Palomar had won him over with her calm and poised attitude that not even an earthquake could shake. Good thing, because people's nerves had always been on edge where Mike was concerned, and matters had only gotten worse since Eunice had joined the shipping agency seven years prior.

Merely weeks after they were hired, Yvette and Palomar struck up a friendship. Who could blame them?

Both beautiful and talented, Eunice had watched them as though they were of a different species. Different from her, to be sure, and in so many ways she hadn't even finished counting them all. Never in her life would Eunice have thought to approach these unreachable creatures, much less talk to them. They could've knocked her down with a feather when Yvette stopped her in the hall one morning and asked her if she wanted to go out for a coffee. Eunice had stuttered that coffee was available on the premises. At Yvette's charming declaration that it tasted like dirty water, Eunice had grabbed her purse and followed her out to a fancy coffee house deep in the French Quarters. The next day, Palomar had joined them, and Yvette had looked mighty pleased as though it were the most natural thing in the world for two Barbie dolls to be hanging out with Moby Dick herself.

It had been the start of a friendship Eunice still marveled at yet cherished beyond anything she'd ever experienced. Not even her parents were as close in her heart as Yvette and Palomar. Then again, Javier and Francine had always been kind of ashamed of their whale-like daughter and hadn't been the most supportive of parents.

Or the most caring.

But that was another story.

"Drinks, girlfriend, remember?" Pinching her arm,

Palomar snapped Eunice out of her reminiscence. "What will you have?"

"Whatever you two are having." It was the safer course of action since she only knew of a couple of cocktails by names and didn't want to seem too unsophisticated. Which she was, no matter how much she tried to hide it.

"We're having the Long Island Iced Tea," Yvette informed her as she moved up the line. "It's a bit strong but very refreshing."

"It's got rum, vodka, tequila, gin, and triple sex." Palomar ticked off the ingredients on her slim fingers without a trace of condescension.

"Fine by me." Extremely glad for her friends' tactfulness, Eunice couldn't wait to try it. "Queen Elizabeth deserves something strong tonight."

"She definitely does." Yvette winked naughtily at her before she combed the room with one of her assessing gazes. "Especially if she gets to meet a handsome prince."

"She's still the virgin here, remember?" Eunice joked.

"Not for long if she's going for a Long Island Iced Tea." Palomar giggled.

"Well, we'll see about that." Unperturbed, Eunice followed Yvette to the table where a Superman barman had begun mixing their drinks.

The man was another muscled hunk who seemed hooked on Palomar, judging from how he was eating her up with eyes alone. Thankfully, he handed Eunice the first drink, so she could scuttle off to leave room for the others in the line to approach the table. Gripping the icy glass, she was so focused on getting out of the way while checking on Yvette and Palomar's whereabouts she wasn't paying attention to where she was going until she hit something-hard, so hard, her wig almost toppled over and fell on the floor.

Confused, her head snapped forward, in time to see her

cocktail spilling all over the sizeable obstacle that had the bad idea of halting her rush. *Boy, did she get mad.*

CHAPTER THREE

"Hey, what's the idea?" Glaring at the stumbling block still anchored to the ground in front of her, Eunice tried to save the last drops of her cocktail. "Can't you watch where you're going?" That technically it was her fault didn't register.

"Forgive me, Your Majesty." The impediment now moved in a deep bow that dripped liqueur to the floor and made the whole thing look silly. "My mistake. I didn't see you coming." Then, all silliness faded as the hurdle straightened itself in all its glory.

A man. That was who she'd bumped, but not just any man.

At first glance, she thought he was cute.

Upon a more thorough examination, she knew he was the stuff women fell in love with all the time.

He was gorgeous.

No, he was magnetic.

Something about him didn't allow her gaze to waver, no matter how much she wanted to steer clear of him. Something inevitably brought it back and refused to let go, not even to blink.

Amazed and scared at the same time, Eunice ogled him without being able to stop herself.

"Please, let me offer you another drink since this came to an untimely end." He smiled, and it was like the entire world had brightened in spite of the candle lights. "What were you drinking, My Queen?"

"Hem . . ." Startled, she jumped back as if coming out of a

dream. "It's all right." Realizing her bad manners had taken the better of her, Eunice composed herself. "I'm the one who should be sorry, and you don't owe me anything."

"I insist, Milady." For good measure, he grabbed her hand.

She had no choice, no choice except sink into purple eyes that promised delights and pleasures beyond her wildest dreams.

"It's obvious it's all my fault." Both firm and proprietary, his squeeze seemed to urge her to acknowledge him fully.

Which she did.

From the exaggerated tilt needed simply to glance at his eyes, she guessed he was six feet five or six. Muscular without the body-builder inflated torso, he had a masculine face with a square jaw, high cheekbones, straight nose, and full lips. His dark complexion blended well with the shoulder-length, thick black hair, but what kept her glued to her spot were his purple eyes that seemed transfixed on her.

"What can I get you?" Gently, he let go of her hand and grabbed her nearly empty glass. "This looks like Long Island Iced Tea." Bringing it to his nose, he sniffed it. "Smells like it, too."

"Yes, it's Long Island Tea." Shaking herself out of whatever confusion this incident had thrown her, Eunice nodded. "But you don't have to worry about it, Mister . . ."

She searched his face for a name that didn't seem to be forthcoming. Then, her gaze dropped to his outfit, and a shiver ran down her back. Maybe, it was her impression, but his tuxedo and black tie reminded her of a vampire she'd seen in a popular TV show. The sensation was further heightened by the nineteen-century-style top hat that sat so elegantly on his head and made him look older, nearly ancient given the drawn lines on his face.

"Count Dracula to your rescue, my dear Queen Elizabeth." Flipping off his hat with his free hand, he went for another curtsy. "If you can wait here for a moment, I'll get you the new drink."

"Yes." Breathless, she couldn't think straight until someone nudged her on the right side, and she realized that she was in the middle of the chamber. "No, actually, I'll wait over there." She pointed at a faraway corner. "I wouldn't want to run into more mishap while you're gone."

"Smart move." He approved, beaming. "It won't take long." He headed toward the bar where another long line was waiting to be sated.

Navigating the crowds in her cumbersome attire was no easy task, though she managed to accomplish it with a good deal of push and shove. Once she reached her destination, she conquered a position with her back right against the wall.

Such had always been her spot on those rare occasions when she'd been invited to parties. Never one to mingle, she'd usually spent her time watching others dance, drink, talk, and have fun. Not anyone's problem if she was rooted to her spot, terrified to leave it to be precise, as though danger lurked just beyond, as though hell might swallow her whole if she dared to budge.

Now, again, she was up against a wall.

Only, this time, it would be different.

She was sure of it.

"Hey, babe, quite a catch!" Bubbling in her happiness, Yvette elbowed her side. "Who's the hunk?"

"Count Dracula," Eunice provided. "It's too bad I had to spill all my drink to get his attention."

"Way to go, girl!" Palomar laughed out loud. "You're finally learning the right moves."

"How to get a man to notice you." Yvette beamed approvingly.

"You think I did it on purpose?" Unsure if that was the lesson, Eunice glanced at her friends.

"Who cares?" Palomar shrugged. "The result is what counts."

"He's buying you another drink, isn't he?" Yvette argued reasonably.

"Don't you think he's a bit old?" Eunice wondered skeptically, remembering her feeling that he wasn't exactly young, not if compared to her thirty years.

"So what?" Yvette was quick to block her. "He doesn't look a day older than fifty."

"Isn't that too old?" Eunice insisted.

"Chica, twenty-years difference is simply perfect." Palomar smirked knowingly. "He looks like Mister Wonderful, and he'll know what to do under the sheets."

Eunice peered at the count stuck in the long line. "Yes, but—"

"No buts." Palomar pressed two long fingers on her mouth. "What's important is that he's going to come back."

"Yeah, and we'll split as soon as he does," Yvette confirmed, fixing a point near the entrance.

Following her focus, Eunice noticed Superman bouncer entering and scanning the chamber as though searching for someone.

"Right." Taking a sip from her drink, Palomar turned her head toward the table at the opposite side, and Eunice could swear she intercepted a knowing look from the barman who had served them earlier. "We have to reel in our own superheroes."

Unlike Yvette, Palomar didn't advertise her personal life. Despite being her friend, Eunice only knew she wasn't in a steady relationship, nor was she sleeping with her boss. At the office, though, everyone wondered how she'd managed to tame Mike Walgate. Palomar had so fiercely denied any sexual involvement that Eunice had no problem believing her. Nor did Yvette. As for the others, they could blab their mouths off until they were black and blue in their face for all Eunice cared about them and their sickly gossip. If it didn't connect any dots about the Creole's romantic life, it didn't matter. Her life was nobody's business except her own, and Eunice had no wish to get any details if none were offered.

"Are you sure you don't want to meet him first?" She spotted Count Dracula at the counter, talking to a bartender. "Just to check him out?"

The fact that either Yvette or Palomar were so attractive that they might've easily stolen this elusive catch of hers didn't even cross her mind. All at once, she felt absurdly nervous about having to face him again and alone.

"Oh, you're sweet." Yvette squeezed her shoulder as if to give her the strength to face him. "But it isn't necessary."

"Yeah, he looks all right," Palomar added her dose of assurance. "And you'll be here just talking to him, right?"

"What if he asks for something more?" Suddenly afraid, she clasped both Yvette and Palomar's hands.

"Honey, the only thing he could ask for more is some good old-fashioned sex." Palomar patted her hand reassuringly. "That could only be good for you." She smiled encouragingly. "Didn't we tell you tonight you'd strike gold?"

"If you don't want it, stay here." Yvette seemed to take her fears more seriously. "We'll come get you at the end of the evening, and we can all share a cab home."

"At what time?" Eunice had no qualms in asking since it was better to be safe than sorry.

"How about three?" Palomar suggested, glancing at her watch.

"It's eleven-thirty now." Eunice checked her Cartier, a graduation gift from her parents, and wondered whether she'd make it that far.

"Let's make it two," Yvette interjected. "If anyone wants to split sooner by herself, just send a text to the other two.

Okay?"

"Great." Palomar was definitely on board with the plan.

As was Eunice. "All right." She exhaled in relief. "Thanks, girls."

They had all come together in a cab, after all, not wanting their driving to interfere with their drinking. It made sense they should all return together unless one of the three got lucky and wanted to end the party in a horizontal position.

Not that she should be worried about it. The way things went with her, she'd be the one calling the cab and returning home alone.

CHAPTER FOUR

"Here you go." Smiling broadly, Count Dracula handed Eunice a brand-new Long Island Iced Tea. "Aren't your friends staying?" He angled his head toward Yvette and Palomar's swaying backsides.

"No, they've got some catching up to do." Feeling him way too close for comfort, she gulped down much of her drink.

The taste was fabulous. The liquid slipped down her throat as cool and refreshing as ice cream in the middle of August, but as treacherous as Eve's apple in the Garden of Eden. She could already feel it working its mischief in her empty belly where butterflies had been gathering on account of Count Dracula's proximity.

"Like it?" The intriguing purple eyes seemed to flash in understanding.

"Absolutely." Ignoring her fluttering stomach, she guzzled another generous sip. "It's my first time with a Long Island Tea, and I know it won't be my last." She giggled uneasily, wondering if she could still retreat before she made a complete fool of herself.

Not that she wanted to for real.

"Good," said the most handsome man in the world to Miss Fatness of the Year. "'Cause I'm planning on spending a lot of time getting to know you better."

"Me?" Nah, she mustn't have heard right. "You wanna get to know *me*?"

"Yes, Your Highness." His deep smile reached his eyes and made them sparkle. "I want to know all there is to know about

19

you."

"Well, shall I start with my family?" Another draw of the dwindling cocktail was in order since her courage was waning.

"That's where it all starts, doesn't it?" He took a swig of his drink, something red and dense.

"How true." She bit her lower lip, unwilling to dwell on Javier and Francine's poor job in raising her. "Well, you've probably heard of my father, Henry." If he wanted to play, she was ready to dazzle him silly, given all the history she'd memorized in school.

"Oh, yes, I'm familiar with good old Henry the Eighth." The way he said it sounded like he'd known the long-deceased sovereign.

For real!

"I mean, who hasn't heard of him?" Now, it seemed he wanted to dispel her impression. "He was a jolly fellow—"

"Not when it came to his wives," she retorted tartly.

"Oh, them." He waved a hand in the air as though her argument was negligible. "He had a bit of a temper." He chuckled. "That's all."

She went on the offensive. "My mother didn't appreciate this *temper* of his."

Whatever her faults, poor Anne Boleyn hadn't deserved to end as she did.

"Your mother lost her head for him," he sneered as though goading her. "In every sense possible."

"That doesn't make it right." She huffed, getting all worked up over her convictions. "Nor excusable."

"Let's say he was a king with an agenda of his own." His soothing tone had a calming effect. "And—"

"She wasn't on it." Eunice laughed, relaxing her stance.

"Women seldom were in those days," he confirmed. "Wives, especially."

"King Henry the Eighth was an autocrat who thought he

could do as he pleased all the time." She reviewed her knowledge about the Tudors, a subject that had fascinated her during her school years. "I'm mighty glad his legacy was mostly carried out by the women he left behind."

"Yes, his daughters proved to be quite effective," he conceded.

"I think they did it only to spite him." She chortled.

"I'm sure they were both pretty mad with the way he treated their mothers." He grinned.

"Yeah, both of them must've been furious." She had no problem imagining Mary or Elizabeth's resentment at an overbearing father who had made their mothers' lives so miserable and tragic.

"That's also what made them such unique queens," he pointed out as though he'd managed to outwit her. "Take Bloody Mary, for instance. If that bigot of Catherine of Aragon hadn't raised her, she would've never embarked in her crusade against the protestants."

"Are you trying to tell me that losing her mother was the best thing that could happen to Elizabeth?" She regarded him with suspicion.

"I'm not saying it was the best thing, but it certainly shaped Elizabeth into becoming one of the greatest monarchs of all time." His logic seemed inescapable. "This is why our family experiences are so crucial and often determine our future."

Then I'm screwed. "Oh, really?" She applied some effort to make it sound disinterested and offhand.

"Definitely." Tipping back his glass, he finished his cocktail. "Your Majesty is as much the product of her dysfunctional parents as of her time."

"Is that why she remained a virgin?" The naughty innuendo slipped out before she was aware of thinking it.

"Nah, she was no virgin." Again, he appeared to possess firsthand knowledge about the Tudors. "That was a myth she fabricated to keep her subjects in check and stop tongues from wagging." He toyed with his empty glass, whirling it between his palms. "Point of fact, she had plenty of lovers, some of which we know because their names circulated despite her tight gag."

"You mean Robert Dudley, Walter Raleigh, Christopher Hatton." Oh, boy, was she glad she had a passion for history! "Or perhaps Robert Devereux."

"Funny you should mention him." Count Dracula surveyed her as though he could read her mind. "Since Your Majesty beheaded him like King Henry beheaded your mother."

"The recurrent family patterns you were talking about." Suddenly, she understood the point he'd been trying to make.

A higher note from a disco blaring from the speaker made her realize she was still in a very crowded chamber at La Maison del Fuego, supposedly to celebrate Halloween. In fact, she was having the best night of her life, not only because conversation came naturally with this stranger. The more they talked, the more she felt like there were only the two of them in the entire world, standing on an enchanted corner all their own.

"Exactly." He beamed at her in satisfaction.

"What makes you such an expert about family patterns, Count Dracula?" Somehow, and despite her earlier reservations, she was getting to like him a lot. "Has all that slaughtering of innocent virgins given you a privileged insight into human nature?"

"For your information, virgins are never innocent." His gaze bore into hers. "They're too full of longing and desire to be the helpless maidens literature wants them to be." He licked his lips smugly. "They lie in bed and fantasize about all the ways a man could love them."

Eunice blushed. "I wouldn't know about that." As incredible as it sounded, this man could be describing her. "I'm not just any virgin." Drawn to him by his magnetic pull, she edged closer. "I'm the Virgin Queen, remember?"

"Hard to forget, Your Majesty." He lowered his voice, forcing her to lean even closer. "Tell me that you don't dream of a stranger doing unspeakable things to you, and I'll leave you alone."

He clasped her around the waist and dragged her until their bodies pressed against one another. Bending, he pressed his lips on her ear. "Tell me that you don't dream of someone feasting on your body like it were candy, of licking the whole of you, of showing you what exquisite pleasure you could feel if only someone took the time to arouse you."

Crap! How can he possibly know? How did he find out about her most secret fantasies?

What he described were the same things she dreamed about every night before she fell asleep, and he was awakening a whole bunch of sensations that would lead her into perdition. The nagging, throbbing of her clit was giving her no respite, nor was the scorching need of a proper nipple pinching.

"I . . ." She swallowed hard, her mind going blank. "I—"

"You don't have to say anything." Placing his empty glass on a nearby table, he squeezed one of her breasts. "Just know that I find you the most beautiful woman I've ever seen."

"Me?" It had to be a joke. "I'm anything but—"

"Hush." He pinned slender fingers on her mouth. "I'm not lying to take you to bed." He sounded so sure of it she had no margins for doubts. "I really think you're quite extraordinary."

Before she had a chance to reply, his lips were on hers. Softly at first, they pressed more decisively until his tongue managed to slip through her defenses. Sweeping her mouth like it belonged to him, he invaded her consciousness in such an erotic way she had to open wider. She had to have him all.

In a word, she surrendered to him, allowing him to have it all.

It was the end of her.

"You're sweet and hot, baby." Pulling back, he nuzzled her neck. "I can't wait to have you." Despite her bulky attire, he succeeded in clamping her buttocks. "If you'll only agree to be my slave tonight, I'll show you what sex is all about."

His closeness, his hands on her, and his smell clogging her nostrils were too intoxicating for her own good, too intoxicating to refuse him anything.

"Yes, take me. I want to be your slave." As his tongue plunged to her throat, she realized all she wanted was to be taken in his arms and let nature take its course.

And everything else be damned!

CHAPTER FIVE

Eunice's sex life had begun in the high school's parking lot. Jim, an eighteen-year-old senior, had asked her out, and she'd spoiled it all by accepting. Like pretty much everything else in her life, it had been a spur of the moment decision made more out of curiosity than because she felt a particular attraction to the guy. He was cute enough, she supposed, but nothing special.

For the very first date of her life, he'd taken her to a drive-through hamburger joint, bought a couple of happy meals, then steered into the deserted parking lot. As soon as he'd munched the last bite of his hamburger, he had demanded a blowjob.

She had obliged, even if it had meant setting aside her cheeseburger. She'd soon regretted her consent. The cheeseburger had tasted much better than Jim's smelly dick, a big, fat stick that had tried to suffocate her with its sudden lurches to reach her stomach.

No, having to negotiate with the beefy fathead for every breath of air hadn't been all that exciting.

Then again, she'd been a virgin. She'd expected something less frantic and more relaxed. Instead, she'd gotten Jim's hurried procedures, like it was a race or something. Still, a part of her had enjoyed the enslavement.

A sticky moistness had pooled between her legs and dampened her panties. Strange yet pleasurable, she hadn't known what to make of this new sensation that had her clit throbbing after a while.

Not that Jim cared a hoot about her new perceptions.

At her inability to swallow him whole, he had applied the same brusque method of reaching his goal. In short, he had pulled her hair to raise her head, pushed her to lie on the back seat, wrenched up her skirt, and gone for her pussy regardless of the underwear standing in the cock's way. Good thing she'd been wet, or he would've hurt her for real.

Well, that happened anyway the second after he had shoved to get his entire thick length inside her.

Maybe, she should've told him she was a virgin. Maybe, it would've improved her situation.

Or maybe not.

Jim was part of the in-crowd, the one Eunice could never aspire to get admitted to, not even in her wildest dreams. It had been odd enough he'd pick her out of the blue, so she hadn't pressed her luck with any unsolicited confessions.

She'd simply bit her lips, ignored the pain, and waited for his furious pumping to abate into an explosive release. The fool hadn't even had the decency to pull out before squirting his juices all inside her torn tissues, which had gotten her fearing a pregnancy along with all sorts of venereal diseases.

Ha! How she wished that had been the extent of her damage.

As if that hadn't been bad enough, the next day, everybody at school had looked at her and burst out laughing when they hadn't huddled in groups to giggle for hours. It had turned out that Jim had been paying penance for some regrettable misdemeanor, and his punishment had been to have sex with Eunice, the school's fatso, then tell everybody about it.

There could be no describing the humiliation, not since she'd managed to put together the whole story after snatching bits and pieces here and there. She would've gladly died on the spot rather than walking in those packed hallways filled with monsters peeking at her as though she were the most despicable creature in the world or attending classes where teachers couldn't be heard over the loud titters and sniggers.

She'd stuck it out 'till the end of the school day, feigning indifference as if it hadn't concerned her at all. Then, she'd gone home and cried her eyes out for hours. If her parents had heard, they had given no sign, nor had they acted any different at the dinner table.

She'd wiped her tears and returned to school the next day, determined to prove that those idiots didn't have what it took to hurt her for real.

Which luckily for her, they didn't.

As the incident slowly faded from collective memory, she'd understood two fundamental lessons. The first was that she was alone in the world and could count on no one, not even her parents. The second was that she liked rough sex.

Eunice's first time had become a distant memory, considering the years that had since passed. Her vagina hadn't torn. She hadn't become pregnant, nor had she contracted any disease. She'd survived her humiliation, which could all be counted as blessings in disguise.

Her second experience had been a one-night stand with Billy, a guy who'd picked her up in a singles' bar. In some ways, Billy had been a replica of Jim, only older and less sure of himself. Like Jim, he must've been part of the in-crowd when in high school. Unlike Jim, he'd fulfilled his potential for failure so had been drowning his uneventful life inside a bottle ever since.

Eunice couldn't have cared less about him.

All she'd wanted was the sensation of being used by a cock.

Billy hadn't quite been the master-type she'd been looking for, but he hadn't left her wanting in either size or manners. He had the most impressive girth that he tried inside her mouth as soon as they reached her tiny flat. She had trouble holding it in one hand. You can imagine how impossible it had been to swallow it.

Billy hadn't been deterred and had kept pushing her head over the fat crown until suffocation had made her sputter and gag. Unmoved, he had continued to press her, and his dick had found a way past her barriers.

Safe to say, she'd gotten more of it down her throat than she'd expected. The feeling hadn't been bad at all, not judging from the dampness pooling between her legs and sparking a deliciously hot sensation. Thinking of that same shaft impaling her wetness and splitting her open had caused thrilled ripples of delight to course up and down her body.

Of course, Billy's only interest had been how far down his monster could reach. Since it hadn't been far enough, he'd decided to switch his attention to her cunt. In an eerily familiar way, he made her lie on the couch, spread her legs, and aligned his stick to her opening. Like Jim, he had shoved into her without bothering to remove her panties. Like Jim, he hadn't used a condom. Like Jim, he had pumped her as though he'd entered a competition.

For Eunice, though, things had been different.

Ever since Jim, she had practiced and learned a trick or two about her body's response, so she knew what to do to make it better for her. Reaching downward, she'd rubbed her clit hard and fast, and the rewards had been spectacular.

While Billy had been hammering as though his life had depended on it, she'd gotten off on pleasure so intense there was no describing it. Her flesh had quivered from the sudden waves radiating from her center, and a series of orgiastic frenzy had her floating on the wings of pure bliss.

Amazing how good it could feel.

Alone, it hadn't been quite as incredible.

With Billy, it had been heaven.

Too bad, Billy hadn't wanted to repeat his performance. Maybe, the fact he drank too much had something to do with it.

Eunice had tried with a few other men, all one-night stands, all very endowed in the dick department, all very uninterested in setting up any kind of relationship with her.

In short, she'd remained alone and unfulfilled until Count Dracula had come and pushed all her buttons.

All the right ones.

CHAPTER SIX

The hotel room at La Maison del Fuego was cozy yet sumptuous at the same time.

Eunice had never seen such luxury in all her life. The king-size bed was so enormous one could get lost inside it.

Sitting on the comfy-looking mattress, Count Dracula pulled her to him. "Not to worry, petite."

The endearment would've sounded ridiculous coming from any other person. This man, instead, pulled it off with a finesse that lent firm credibility to it.

"I won't let you be lost," he added huskily.

She briefly wondered how this man, a virtual stranger, had talked her into following him here without even sending a message to her girlfriends. Maybe, she should ask him what his real name was, but his hands clutching her ass, then cupping her breasts kind of messed with her priorities until everything not related to sex fled from her mind.

As he kissed her, his tongue leisurely stroked the inside of her mouth without any rush. Like he had all the time in the world, which maybe he had, considering how slowly he went about removing her bulky outfit.

First, the wig that had been such torture. Next, the garment that had emphasized Eunice's resemblance to the blue whale. With slow, unhurried patience, he unlatched the million tiny buttons holding it together. Once the front was open, he pushed down the sleeves and forced the rest of the material to fall to her ankles. Then, it was the corset's turn to be unfastened and removed, leaving her large breasts exposed.

"You are more lovely than I ever imagined."

She believed him without hesitation, for there was no trace of mockery in his voice. Better, there was a trace of reverence in the way he worked the fat mass in front of his mouth and in the way he sucked each nipple in turn.

This treatment was a novelty.

All she'd been used to was an absolute contempt of her physical shape from her few partners. They had used and abused her either because they had to prove something, or she'd made herself available for her own needs. Whatever the reason, they hadn't cared for her reactions as long as she provided what they wanted.

Count Dracula was another matter altogether. His hands moved down to her pubic area. Nimble fingers dug in her crevice from above the panties, starting a dull throb of exquisite desire.

As though he perceived it, he made her lie on the bed, then pressed his face on the spot that was driving her crazy. Without removing the underwear, he nuzzled her clit, playfully at first, nipping it together with the cotton fabric until he guzzled it good and proper. At the same time, his hand pressed on her slit, trying to cram both fingers and undies inside it.

An impossible task, of course, which didn't prevent her arousal from soaring higher than it already had.

Eunice would've died on the spot had the urge to come not interfered with the shocking pleasure of it all.

Unperturbed by the heat he was unleashing so effortlessly, he continued to lavish her cunt with the finesse of a man who obviously loved women. Insisting on licking her drenched swell, he penetrated to her core despite the lingerie standing in the way.

Not content, she tried to accelerate his task by spreading her legs wider and swaying to the rhythm of his fondling. Not that she needed it. She'd become a veritable pool of honeydew, so thick and strong she could smell it from where she lay. It was all the excitement of feeling this man close yet not close enough. It tormented her flesh and kept a barrier that reduced the intensity of the sensation, which of course kept her from climaxing.

Frustrating her at every turn was more like it.

As she was about to protest her latest dissatisfaction, he brushed off the annoying fabric and attacked her bare skin with renewed vigor.

The abruptness of the naked touch drove her to clench her legs and trap him so that he could do nothing except feast on her pussy. When he did just that, she burst so utterly that her convulsions ran for five minutes straight.

Well, maybe less, but who was counting?

She was melting all over that bed and never wanted it to stop.

Ever!

Alas, it did eventually, and it coincided with the moment Count Dracula turned her on her belly. Removing what had become a soaked undergarment, he buried his face in her ass cheeks.

Eunice tensed. Would he ask for anal sex?

"Ah, petite, you've got such a magnificent derriere." He slurped the crack with long, lavish tongue-sweeps. "I'm tempted to take it whether you consent or not."

This statement immediately perked up her masochistic inclination despite her skepticism. "I've never done it," she squealed, confused by her reactions.

"That's not the point." Deliberately, he stuck two fingers in the puckered hole. "The point is, do you want to try it?"

"I'm not sure." The pressure on her back ring didn't seem all that hot, even if she understood there could be more to it than she'd initially assessed.

He chortled. "Then, it'll be my job to make sure you do."

She wasn't sure it would be the excellent idea he seemed to imply.

Then again, she had accepted everything men had done to her, so why not this?

If she expected him to move on it right at the moment, she was sorely disappointed.

As though he'd lost interest in it, Count Dracula's fingers were exploring the damp core of her cunt. In and out they went, increasing the beat until she could stand it no more and lifted her hips to demand something more substantial.

He had no trouble satisfying her.

Something thick and stiff slammed in her pussy, filling it to completion.

No, more than that. It was like this particular dick had been made especially for her. The way it felt inside was sheer perfection. Like it touched the entire available space until not a half-inch of her lacked its firm girth. Like it had glued itself to her skin, the precise dimensions that made it fit like a custom-made glove.

She wished she'd seen this prodigious cock before he'd lodged it inside her welcoming flesh. This one for sure would've deserved her complete adoration had he only requested it. Since he hadn't, she lost herself in his skillful pumping, the fantastic piece ramming her pussy so divinely she found it impossible to hold still.

Thrusting upward, she met his every shove until it seemed like they moved as one.

Which maybe they were because she couldn't tell where he ended and she began.

Oh, crap, would you believe it?

She climaxed again!

Like an unstoppable rush, her body thrashed uncontrollably. In her frenzy, she held nothing back. She let him have it all, as though freed from the constrictions that usually imprisoned her.

The most rewarding effect of her total abandonment was his load spraying to her belly in a series of ecstatic gasps.

Right after, he fell silent, and she tensed.

This stage was usually the one where men dumped her. She knew the drill by heart and half-anticipated Count Dracula to rise, mumble some excuse or other, then get the hell out of there as though she were contaminated or something.

"Boy, you're amazing."

The remark caught her off guard.

No, what surprised her was that he was still stuck to the hilt, as hard as if he hadn't come at all.

"I'd never grow tired of you." He nuzzled her neck.

She wondered if he meant it.

"Of your accommodating cunt." When he wriggled his hips, his shaft had the dimensions of an unsatisfied monster. "I'd stay here forever if your virgin ass wasn't waiting for me."

Oh, shit!

She'd hoped he might've forgotten.

"You can stay if you want." She tried to convince him by squeezing every muscle in her pelvis.

"And miss your great ass?" Chuckling, he straightened and removed his penis from her enlarged pussy. "Not a chance."

Next thing she knew, he fell on her butt as if it were candy.

Digging his fingers in her generous buttocks, he tightened his grip in a fierce squeeze that made her flesh tremble. Her asshole also received its share of attention. From a luscious tongue drill to finger penetration, he coaxed it into total surrender.

She could feel her reservations crumbling under the onslaught. Her physical ones, at least, while her brain still had doubts about the procedure.

"It's no use denying it, ma petite," he mused. "You want it."

Was this guy psychic or something?

Eunice had no idea why he appeared capable of reading her mind. She only knew it was giving him way too many advantages.

"If you say so," she retorted uneasily.

"Of course, I do." Grasping both cheeks, he held them wide apart. "And you've got nothing to fear." He slid his gigantic beast along the cleft. "Now, before I take this delicious morsel, why don't you touch yourself?"

"Touch myself?" Had she heard correctly?

"Yes, so it'll be better for you," he explained with a tone that was full of concern.

"Really?" Well, she was damn impressed.

No one before had ever given a fucking hoot about her well-being. "Does this mean it might hurt?" *Hey, just checking, right?*

"Not with me, petite."

To her ears, it sounded like a lie pure and simple, even if she didn't have the heart to challenge it.

"You'll see."

Yeah, can't wait. Silencing the snappy comeback, Eunice slipped a hand under her stomach and searched for her clit. When she found a puffed-up knot of insatiable craving, he could've knocked her down with a feather. Her body wanted it way more than it had let on so far.

Stroking that sensitive spot only heightened her lust.

He was probably counting on it.

At her first upward swing, his considerable equipment split her in two.

Literally!

Like a nutshell, the force of his impact flung open her narrow entrance with an audible cracking sound.

"Ouch!" Curling on herself, she tried to escape his monster.

He did not allow her. "Relax and breathe deeply," he ordered instead.

Yeah, sure. Count Dracula could talk it up all he liked. He wasn't the one stuck with a baseball bat up his ass.

"I know it can be difficult at first." Leaning on her, he snaked a hand under her belly. "Trust me. It'll be the most amazing orgasm of your life if you just follow my lead." Having found her pussy, he entangled his fingers with hers and caressed the hungry clit swimming in an ocean of velvety moistness.

Well, damn him!

He might be right, after all.

As the burning faded, a new sensation took over and demanded she deepen her touch, which in turn triggered the need for something huge to stuff the very same hole that had been in excruciating pain moments before.

Together, their fingers dipped in the recesses of her slit, caressing the wet folds until she swayed in eager anticipation.

It had to be the signal he'd been expecting, for he removed his hand swiftly, pressed it on the mattress, and pushed his massive piece to her bowels. That was how deep it got with his first shove alone. The ones that followed weren't less gentle. It felt like Count Dracula was rough on purpose, driving his stick so far down she was hanging on for dear life.

And yet, she loved it. Every minute of it brought her closer to the point of no return.

Gone were all the impediments. He was free to indulge himself, and his dick slammed into her yielding flesh as though it hoped to reach her throat from her backside.

Not that she would've been surprised if it had. The way he was screwing it to the guts boosted its chances of success.

Yes, most definitely, she was taking flight. Carried away by her bliss, she soared while wave after wave coiled from the center and shot her to the stars.

Floating up and away, she wasn't aware of her body except in the exquisite pleasure bursting from every pore. Then, just as she thought she'd crash down, it started anew, and she lost all measure of sanity.

The fact he was unloading all over her derriere wasn't helping either.

His rhythm peaked, and she was in for a third ride, moving against him as though there would never be an ending to both their orgasms.

Just wishful thinking, of course.

Regrettably, this new high couldn't last all night long.

The first to recover his wits was Count Dracula, who collapsed on her before rolling to her side.

The second was Eunice herself. Too bad that when she came down from heaven, exhaustion overpowered her. She could barely budge, only enough to wobble on her back to die in peace.

Chapter Seven

"Wow! I'm beat." Unable to suppress a huge yawn, Eunice opened her mouth wide and let it go.

Sprawled naked and sated on the king-size bed that had been her undoing, she wondered why she felt so tired. For sure, she would've gladly slept for a week.

No, actually, she had not the slightest spark of energy, which would've been puzzling had she not felt too weary for any serious conjecture.

It was probably all the sex's fault, but it would've seemed rude had she capsized and gone to sleep. After all that satisfying and entirely unexpected great sex, she owed her Count Dracula a bit more consideration.

"Funny, I had the best time in the world yet don't even know your name." Funny also how Count Dracula seemed younger now, a lad no older than twenty-five rather than the mature man she'd taken him to be at first.

Simply another mystery she wasn't up to uncovering. Keeping her eyes open was an effort in itself.

"Your real name, I mean," she added for the benefit of greater understanding.

Turning to her, he grabbed her hand. "Adrien Ascott, at your service, Your Majesty."

Damn!

Besides being the most skilled lover she'd ever had the pleasure to meet, the man had an impressive name if she said so herself.

"Not a majesty." Limply, she tried squeezing his hand

without too much success. "I'm Eunice Saint Jacques."

"Enchanté, mademoiselle." Adrien, instead, had no trouble clasping her hand with vital force.

"Oh, I don't know too much French." She attempted a giggle that came out as a croak. "My parents never spoke it at home, and I wasn't too good with it at school."

"Too bad, 'cause it's a beautiful language." If he wanted to convince her, he need not.

"I know." She sighed. "But I wasn't too good with foreign languages." Her brain scrambled for something to keep him talking before she dropped off once and for all. "Have you known it long?"

"All my life." His voice became dreamy. "I grew up on the Côte d'Azur —"

"Ah, on the French Riviera." That much she knew even in her muddled state.

"Yes, in Provence, to be precise." Gently, he caressed her face. "In a town that's called Aix-en-Provence."

"In Provence, you say?" That tidbit, instead, was news to her. "Never heard of it."

"It's one of the best regions in France." His voice grew husky. "Next to the sea and the hills. Summer is the best season ever. It's a feast for the eyes with ripe fields everywhere, a sea that defines the horizon, and the sky big enough to swallow everything, sea included." He paused to take a breath. "The air, ah, the air is fantastic. It's sweet and fragrant and smells of lavender. All you can hear are grasshoppers singing their hearts out all day long like they're holding a festival or something." He chuckled. "We love them so much they've become the symbol of Provence, along with lavender."

"Sounds lovely," she slurred in fatigue. "Did you have a girlfriend there?" Crap, why had she asked that?

She wasn't really interested, only didn't want to fall asleep just yet.

"Nah, I had many women." He grinned, and she imagined his face lighting up through her half-closed eyes. "Never have been one to settle down."

"You mean you never fell in love?" With an effort, she opened her eyes to stare at him in amazement.

"Well, it might've happened once or twice . . ."

From the way he trailed off, she guessed it wasn't something he liked to share. "Oh, do tell." She pouted, hoping the story would be long enough for her to doze off without feeling too guilty.

"Not much to tell." Stretching out, Adrien placed his arms under his head. "Like I said, I was born in Provence. My family was of noble descent, but a prominent name was all that was left when I showed up. The money and prestige had been gambled away in a series of bad investments."

He paused as though reliving the bitterness of such a loss. "My father was a farmer, and my mother stayed home to care for the family. I had ten sisters and brothers, so you can imagine."

Big family, was her thought as she drifted toward the unconscious. It wasn't something you heard of these days.

"Anyway, my old man wanted us to learn a trade. Since I loved animals, I became a stable hand and soon was employed by a noble family, called Le Clerque," he continued. "They were mighty and wealthy. They also had a daughter, Julia, who fell hopelessly in love with me."

"Did you love her?" Somehow, curiosity roused her enough to ask the question.

"I thought I did." There was a trace of sadness Eunice couldn't entirely ignore. "Julia was younger than me, enchanting yet immature. She was eighteen while I was twenty-one years old. I had already sampled some of the female delights of my region, but I had to admit that she was different."

"Different in what way?" Eunice wondered out loud.

"She was sweet and innocent," he offered.

"You told me that virgins are never innocent," she teased.

"Julia was the exception that proves the rule," he retorted. "I'd go as far as saying she was pure and without malice when I first met her."

"Then, she was a virgin," was Eunice's inevitable conclusion.

"Oh, yes, she was a virgin." Lazily, he dragged himself to a half-sitting position and flicked nimble fingertips on her nipples.

The treacherous louts responded immediately, perking up as though they hadn't had their fill yet.

"Aha, someone's still in a mood." Before she could protest, his warm mouth grazed the taut buds, his tongue drowning them in wet kisses. "You remind me of her." Raising his head, he trailed up to her ear. "For one thing, she was as beautiful as you are."

"You mean fat, right?" Despite her weariness, she couldn't keep the aggressive edge off her voice.

"You aren't fat, my dear." Caressing her face, he slid on top of her. "You are soft." His mouth descended on hers, and talking became the last item on his agenda.

Nudging a knee between her legs, he created enough space to slip his colossal beast inside her pussy. Exactly when it had become so thick and rigid, Eunice had no idea. She knew she welcomed it, spreading her legs further until he was embedded to the root.

"I spent a great deal of time with Julia, teaching her all about sex." He set an unhurried and slow rhythm. "I took advantage of her beautiful body whatever way I could until I enslaved her."

"Are you sure it wasn't she who enslaved you?" Even if she wasn't thinking too clearly, she wanted to challenge his certainties.

The man stopped moving altogether and cupped her face. "I never considered it that way."

"You should." She raised her cunt to convince him to resume the screwing before exhaustion overtook her.

"Yeah, I should." Taking the hint, he accelerated the beat.

Soon, he was shoving in and out as if his life depended on it. Eunice matched him thrust for thrust while her clit rubbed on his pubic area, which felt so divine she knew she couldn't hold it together for much longer.

Her first orgasm caught her unaware. Adrien had just drilled his entire spectacular length in the whole of her slit when she burst.

Frantic convulsions gripped her full in the flesh, trapping his dick and refusing to let it go.

The second wave of pure bliss closely followed the first one, or maybe it was all one giant come.

That was also when he came, reclining on her to shoot his seed to her belly, which spurred her new round of pleasure. Tightening her legs around his waist, she rode out the unraveling of her senses until nothing was left except a vast emptiness.

This time, it was definitely over, and she collapsed. Etiquette or no etiquette, she would bid Adrien goodnight, and who cared if he found it rude.

"This has been wonderful." An indecent gasp escaped her lips. "By the way, what happened to Julia?"

"Oh, we parted ways a long, long time ago." His fingers raked through her hair. "I haven't seen her since."

"I see." Straining herself for the final time, she turned on a side. "But now, I'm drained." Her mouth gaped from the potency of another yawn. "I hope you don't mind if I take a quick nap."

"No, go right ahead. I'll be here when you wake up." It was the last thing she heard before darkness swallowed her.

CHAPTER EIGHT: YVETTE

"Uh, baby, you're the best." Tony Spencer's admiration was directed to her backside, splayed as it was on his desk.

Open and vulnerable, Yvette Carlisle knew that was how her boss liked her best. Holding the cheeks apart before ravaging them was a way to get his dick ready for the ensuing possession.

"Are you nice and wet for me?" Tony's husky breath pierced her thick fog of lust.

"Yes, Master." *How could I not?*

The cock sliding in between her crack was pure perfection.

No, it was sublime, and it was driving her crazy, liquefying her insides worse than when he'd slammed her on the desk after calling on her secretarial services. A seemingly innocent request, the excuse of having to dictate an important letter, and she'd fallen straight into his trap. One moment, she'd been walking into his spacious, all-windows corner office looking out from the twentieth floor. The next, a harsh and unyielding boss had tackled her down to the floor. His fly already open, he had her choke on a stone-like piece whose only aim was total suffocation.

Yvette hadn't minded at all.

It was taking her mind off the nagging question of what had happened to Eunice. For the first time ever, she hadn't shown up for work. Maybe, her evening with Mister Wonderful dressed as Count Dracula had been too much for her, and she was resting at home. It could explain why she hadn't answered any of the texts Yvette and Palomar had been sending her since the end of the Halloween party, nor had she picked up when they had phoned. Strange, though, because the calls hadn't gone to voice mail, which meant the phone wasn't dead or anything.

"I don't believe you." As though sensing she'd slipped away, Tony enforced his skepticism by sticking three fingers in her narrow ring and twisting them mercilessly.

Again, nothing she couldn't handle.

She loved this rough treatment from the man she'd chosen as her master.

Sure, he was married and had tons of other women on the side. He was also one of the hottest players in the New Orleans club scene, given his good looks, money, and influence.

She had realized it when she'd applied for a job at the renowned Goldblum Freight Services. She hadn't been the only one after the position, of course.

A considerable collection of women aspiring to become Tony Spencer's secretary had greeted her in the large waiting room. The moment her gaze had connected with Tony's steely one, Yvette had known the job would be hers because she could be so much more than a regular secretary.

Which was what he'd been looking for, a beautiful, compliant slave to keep around the office.

Well, she had the looks and the inclination.

In short, she had all the qualifications for this tall, six feet three, perfect hunk of a god that was Tony Spencer and his demanding requirements.

"Prove it."

Tony's order didn't catch her by surprise. She'd been expecting it from the moment he'd decided a blowjob wouldn't satisfy him.

No, no matter how good she was in swallowing him, he always craved something more than his cock down her throat.

That had been when he'd brutally ripped her ultra-fine thongs and thrown them in the wastebasket. Later, she'd have to dip into her desk drawer to get a new pair. Good thing his abuse didn't stop at her underwear.

Her clit hammering furiously reminded her that she hadn't yet complied with his order. She plunged two fingers in her incredibly bare and exceedingly drenched cunt. "Here, Master." She twisted her arm up and behind. "Taste me."

He sucked her fingers. "Delicious." For good measure, he lapped them one more time. "But it could stand some improvement."

Before she had the chance to think about how he might like it better, he jabbed her pussy with a thick-sized dildo that enlarged her all at once.

All together, too.

"There." He adjusted the fit by impaling the toy to the root. "Much better." Leaning heavily on her flat belly squashed on the wooden surface, he spread her buttocks further apart. "Now, I can take this sweet bottom of yours."

Yvette relaxed, ready for impact. Since he hadn't forbidden her to touch herself, her fingers started a circular rub of her impatient clit.

When the fathead lined up with her puckered hole, she intensified her stroking. As the constraint increased, her front space shrank even more until there wasn't a part of her that was empty.

Next thing she knew, Tony was balls-deep in her ass.

He filled it all, no question about it.

She loved it all, no question about it.

The double pressure of dick and dildo drove her crazy every time.

It was uncanny yet blissful at the same time.

Tony was a master in pumping her butt. He slid in and out as though his piece had been built for just such a job, for just such a space as hers.

With a precise beat, he blew her backside to bits, also juggling the considerable stuffing planted in her slit. The combination of her fingers digging in her cunt was the extra turn-on that was about to make her fly.

"Who gave you permission to touch yourself?" The low growl didn't sound like Tony at all.

"Hem . . ." She knew she was stalling for time. "You . . ." She was close. So close, she had no intention of stopping the sensual titillation.

Getting ready to face the consequences of her disobedience, she took a deep breath. "You didn't say I couldn't."

"You didn't ask, slut." Tony's hoarse comeback was a sure sign he was about to unload.

This new awareness made her stick to her insubordination. After another deep fondling of her burning swell, she nailed it.

"Bitch!" Evidently understanding he was too late, he thrust his entire length inside her wide-open derriere and increased his pounding.

She could care less.

She was coming all over the place.

As was he, his ragged breath unable to hide the explosion of creamy cum filling her ass.

His release heightened hers.

She came again, the waves of pleasure radiating from her center to the tips of her toes.

"You fucking bitch." Pulling out of her ass, he slapped her on her buttock, hard and fierce.

Since this was all part of their relationship, she didn't try to stop him. "Master, please, I didn't think that—"

"Shut up, slut." He spanked her again. "When your master orders, you don't think." His flat palm struck her backside one more time. "You obey."

As he raised his arm, the intercom buzzed, and he had to stretch over her to answer it.

Saved by the bell, or so she hoped, Yvette perked up her ears.

"Yes?" Tony growled.

"Mister Spencer." The female voice at the other end could only be Claudia's, the latest intern. "The police are here, and they're asking for a moment of your time."

CHAPTER NINE

"Please, come in, officers." After having redressed in haste, Yvette gestured for the man and woman waiting outside the door to advance. "Mister Spencer will see you now."

"Thank you." The woman approached the desk. "I'm Sergeant Regina Kirkpatrick of the NOPD." She flashed a badge. "This is my partner, Officer Carlos Perez."

The man also held a police ID.

Yvette was about to step out when a cold sensation gripped her stomach. "Forgive me, officers, does this have something to do with Eunice?" It came out before she could stop herself.

"Who might you be?" The detective woman narrowed her gaze on her.

"I'm Yvette Carlisle." She introduced herself. "Tony Spencer's secretary and—"

"You know Eunice Saint Jacques?" Regina Kirkpatrick's demeanor didn't alter a bit, steeped as it was in evident distrust.

"Yes, of course, we're friends, not just colleagues." Yvette's stomach felt even queasier. "We went out last night to celebrate Halloween, but today she hasn't shown up for work." Which was as unusual as the sky falling over and burying New Orleans. "We sent her several texts." Panic rising, her voice trembled, "When she didn't answer, we tried calling her several times—"

"We?" Regina Kirkpatrick lifted a quizzical eyebrow.

"Yes, Palomar and I," Yvette provided. "We've been worried—"

"Who's Palomar?" It was Officer Carlos Perez's turn to look at her with suspicion.

Yvette groaned inwardly. All these questions didn't seem relevant to the real issue of what had happened to Eunice.

Then again, these police officers were probably just doing their job while she allowed her anxiety over her friend to get the better of her. She mentally counted to ten, then took a deep breath. "Palomar Redondo is Mike Walgate's secretary and another friend of Eunice."

"She works here, too?" Carlos Perez didn't seem to have heard her at all.

Is the guy dumb or something? "Yes, she works here, too," Yvette assented wearily, wondering whether she should stop volunteering information and concentrate on answering their stupid questions.

Detective Kirkpatrick picked up the earlier thread. "Tell us exactly why you and Palomar have been worried."

"Excuse me." Clearing his throat, Tony had both officers spin toward him. "If you don't mind, I didn't know this Eunice all that well."

Not a lie. For her boss, Eunice had been the company's fatso, and he'd never bothered with the likes of her.

"And I've got work to do." He smiled in a blatant attempt to make the police understand his predicament. "As of now, Yvette is instructed to give her full cooperation, and you can use one of our meeting rooms for whatever other questions you might have."

"You really don't know Eunice Saint Jacques?" Sergeant Regina sized him up with one scornful glance. "Aren't you General Manager of Goldblum Freight Services?" It was obvious she'd done her homework. "Shouldn't you know all your employees?"

"Detective Regina, do you have any idea of how many people Goldblum employs?" Tony's smile was a little strained.

"About five hundred." Carlos threw the figure at him as though he'd pulled up everything there was to know about the company.

"Do you honestly expect me to know all of them?" Tony challenged.

The officers exchanged a glance before returning their gazes on her boss.

"I suppose not," Regina relented at last. "Where did you say the meeting rooms were?"

"Down the hall." Tony vaguely indicated outside his door.

To Yvette, who knew him quite well, he was trying to suppress a grin of satisfaction at having gotten rid of the police so quickly.

"Yvette will take you." It sounded like a dismissal. "While I instruct Kerry, our Chief of Human Resources, to give you a copy of Eunice's personnel file, in case you should need it."

"Yes, we probably will," Kirkpatrick conceded. "Thank you, Mister Spencer." A slight nod, then she turned to Yvette. "Shall we go?"

"Yes, this way." Stepping through the threshold, she walked briskly toward the farthest meeting room, all the while wondering what had happened to Eunice.

The police had offered no clue, and she was determined to find out sooner rather than later.

Arriving at the destination, she held the door open and watched as the two officers marched in then sat together on one side of the long table. Naturally, she settled on the opposite side so that it looked like a classic interrogation setup.

"Now, Miss Carlisle, tell us exactly why you and Palomar have been worried." Leaning on her arms, Regina Kirkpatrick stretched forward as if she wanted to grab her.

"No." Laying her new smartphone on the table, Yvette went on the offensive. "First, you tell me what happened to Eunice." She didn't care if this was the police, if she sounded rude, or if she'd become a suspect.

The conviction that something terrible must've happened to Eunice was gaining strength with every passing moment since these two imbeciles had walked into Tony's office. The pressure was getting to her.

The two didn't precisely scramble to reply.

They merely stared at her until Yvette squirmed with real unease.

Finally, Carlos Perez opened his mouth. "I'm sorry to inform you that your friend has died."

CHAPTER TEN

"**W**hat?" Nah, Yvette probably hadn't heard correctly. "Died?" *It couldn't be! Just couldn't!* "There must be a mistake. Eunice was fine yesterday. We were together last night at this party, and she was enjoying herself."

"The Eunice we're talking about was thirty years old, on the chubby side, and she lived in . . ." Officer Carlos dug out of a pocket a piece of paper and rattled off an address and a telephone number.

They were Eunice's all right.

Defeated, Yvette felt the tears stinging her eyes, and she didn't try to stop them. "I don't understand," she bawled. "Are you sure it's her?"

"Pretty sure." Sergeant Kirkpatrick nodded. "Though we've asked Mister Javier Saint Jacques to identify her later today."

At the mention of Eunice's dad, Yvette's blood went icy cold. "How-how," she stuttered, unable to think clearly. "How did she die? Where did you find her?"

"From our preliminary findings, it seems to be of heart attack," Regina supplied softly. "We'll get to the where later."

"Heart attack?" It was news to her. She sniffled. "She never had any problems with her heart."

"It's not unusual for people of her weight to have heart trouble." There was an edge to Officer Perez's voice that she didn't like at all.

"Are you saying she's fat?" Yvette hissed.

"I'm only saying she didn't seem in top shape." Carlos

shrugged, indifferent.

"You're wrong, detective." A fresh wave of sadness washed over her. "She was fine last night," she repeated stubbornly as though it could have the power to bring back Eunice.

"I'm deeply sorry for your loss, Miss Carlisle."

Regina Kirkpatrick's empathy must've kicked in. Yvette felt a wave of something similar to sympathy emanate from the woman.

"You two were close?"

"Yes, she was my best friend." Yvette wiped her eyes with the back of her hand, then looked for a tissue inside the lining in her skin-tight miniskirt.

"Were you?" Regina's dubious expression said how little she believed her. "We couldn't help noticing that you don't exactly look alike."

"So what?" Yvette flared. "You think that just because she was chubby, I couldn't be her friend?" It was kind of clear that they did. "Eunice is a sweet, innocent girl who hasn't been too happy in her life." She felt like crying all over again. "She's a wonderful person and great fun to be around." She blew her nose. "I didn't like how life had treated her. I suppose that's what drew me to her."

"When did you first meet her?" Regina seemed keen to know.

"Three years ago." The memory of it was as sharp as though it had happened yesterday. "When Mister Spencer hired me, Eunice had been working as an accountant for something like seven or eight years."

Yvette remembered seeing her at her desk in the solitary office from which she seldom ventured out like she'd been a hermit or something. Then again, people hadn't been exactly friendly with her. Sure, everyone knew she was a competent professional, quite skilled at what she did, but they could care

less. All they saw was a plump person with relationship is-
sues, so most of them offended her behind her back.

The company fatso.

That was how they called her whenever she wasn't around,
though she'd probably heard them.

"People had been mean to her." Yvette shook her head
wryly. "She hadn't too many friends when I got here."

"Calling her names behind her back, I bet." Carlos Perez
was quick to connect the dots.

"Yeah, something like that." Once Yvette had learned all
the sordid details of how Goldblum treated its star accountant, she'd been enraged for Eunice's sake. A couple of weeks
after being hired, she'd walked into Eunice's office and asked
her out for coffee. "That was just the beginning of our friendship." She smiled, remembering some of the wild weekends
they had spent together. "I soon discovered how unique
Eunice is, with a mind and a personality all her own, capable
of standing up to the worst things that life can throw at you."
Like awful parents and classmates. "She's also intelligent and
quite funny with a great sense of humor. That's why I tried to
be close to her."

"Was it easy?" Regina inquired.

"Well, not at first," Yvette had to admit.

Eunice had been taken aback, no question about it, but
Yvette's insistence had won her over eventually.

"You have to understand that she's . . ."

Oh, my God! Eunice is no more! The awareness hit her like a
blow to the stomach. "I mean . . ." Strenuously, Yvette pulled
herself together, for it wouldn't do to fall apart in front of the
police. "She was so much more than I've been telling you, so
different from anyone I've ever known, sensitive, kind, and
full of hope, but also shy and introverted."

Knowing how terrifying people were for Eunice, Yvette
had never pressed her. Instead, she'd given her friend all the
time she needed to adapt, taking care of all the small talk and

invitations until Eunice had eased into friendship. "It took some time and convincing, but we became friends and spent a great deal of time together."

"Also outside of the office?" Detective Regina fixed her intently.

"Yes, especially outside of the office." Yvette nodded. "We went out a lot, mostly to dinner and pubs, but last night we got invited to this exclusive Halloween party—"

"Yes, tell us about the party." Flipping out a notepad and a pencil, Officer Perez was ready for business. "What time did you get together? Who else was with you?"

"Start at the beginning if you don't mind," Detective Kirkpatrick interjected. Gone was the caring façade. She seemed to be sharpening her claws for some serious cross-examination. "Did you see Eunice at work yesterday?"

"Yes, we usually have coffee at eleven." Distractedly, she glanced at her watch and noticed it was already noon.

"Who do you mean by *we*?" Hard at work, Carlos was jotting something down.

"Palomar, Eunice, and I." *Unbelievable how thickheaded these cops could be.* "We always take our break together and go—"

"Palomar Redondo, right?" Officer Carlos interrupted her.

"Yes, her." Yvette rolled her eyes impatiently.

"Where do you go for coffee around here?"

Regina's attempt at a smile was more of a smug smirk. The woman was probably enjoying her discomfort. There could be no other explanation. Taking a grip, Yvette braced herself for an extensive interview.

"We always go to Joe's, which is around the corner."

"Does Miss Redondo usually join you?" Officer Perez's pencil remained poised in midair.

"Yes, she does," Yvette confirmed. "She's also one of Eunice's friends, and the three of us have been going out together ever since Palomar and I joined this company."

Perhaps, she was repeating herself and providing too much detail. Carlos wrote down everything anyway, and she noticed he was left-handed.

"So . . ." Detective Regina pursed her lips. "You met both Miss Saint Jacques and Miss Redondo when you were hired as a secretary for Goldblum." It sounded more like a statement than a question, which didn't mean Yvette could ignore it.

"Yes, I did."

"I see." Sergeant Kirkpatrick glanced at her partner's notes before continuing, "What did you do after coffee?"

"We worked until five." Yvette didn't need any more prompts to resume her story. "We all left together 'cause we had to pick up our Halloween costumes, go to the beautician, and get ready for the party."

She remembered how thrilled they had all been — yes, even Eunice — and a fresh tear slid down her face. "Sorry." She wiped it away with the tissue and blew her nose again. "We were all looking forward to it."

"Where was the party?" Officer Perez peered at her.

"At La Maison del Fuego, the famous hotel in the French Quarter." One of her legs was cramping. She shifted position.

"What time did you get there?" Regina straightened on her high-back chair.

"We went around . . ." Yvette creased her forehead, trying to remember the exact time. "It must've been around eleven." She reviewed the evening in her head. "We had gone to dinner around seven-thirty."

"Where?" Carlos Perez looked ready to add another line to the already crammed page of his notepad.

"We went to Chez Martin."

Nervously, Yvette played with the slim white-gold collar Tony had given her during the summer. She hadn't wanted one because she liked to play the field and didn't want to be tied down to one master alone. He had insisted, telling her she was free to screw whomever she liked. It turned out he didn't need a sub. He had plenty of them and found them rather dull after a while. He wanted a slave with her own mind when she wasn't having sex. A slave he encouraged to get screwed by others, only they had to know she belonged to him. His only requirement was to wear it around the office and at Sortilege, his BDSM club.

"It's the new place downtown," she explained. "You know, it's right around —"

"Yes, we're familiar with Chez Martin." From the way Detective Kirkpatrick said it, she guessed the woman must've already eaten there. "What time did you finish dinner?"

"It must've been nine or nine-thirty." For the life of her, Yvette couldn't remember precisely. "Then, we all went to Eunice's flat and got dressed up." She almost smiled, remembering how hard it had been to squeeze all together into such a tiny place.

"Y'all managed to fit?" Carlos sneered.

Definitely, Officer Perez didn't seem to have too much liking for poor Eunice.

"We did." *You prick.* "Even if it was a bit cramped." Yvette's gaze snagged to Regina Kirkpatrick, who seemed less of an asshole. "We didn't have to stay long, anyway. We had to get dressed, and then we left for the hotel."

"Who drove?" Evidently wanting to recapture her attention, Carlos stretched forward.

"No one." However, overwhelming the temptation to ignore him, Yvette knew better than to follow it. "We took a cab." She regarded the man coldly. "We wanted to drink at the party and figured it was best to avoid any driving."

"Wise decision," Regina approved, inclining her head.

"What was your plan on returning home?" Piqued, Officer Perez stared at her with palpable hostility.

Yvette's lips curved upward in a falsely sweet smile. "We were planning on sharing another cab."

No, she absolutely didn't like Officer Perez.

"Did you have a particular deadline for calling this other cab?" Carlos growled.

"Yes." To hide her dislike, Yvette toyed with her mobile. "We were planning on leaving around two." She sighed, wishing things had gone according to plan. "If one of us wanted to stay behind, she would've sent a text to the other two, so we wouldn't worry."

"Did Eunice send such a text?" Detective Kirkpatrick pressed.

"No, she didn't." All of a sudden, Yvette realized where they had found Eunice. "Oh, my God!" *That bastard of a Count Dracula must have a lot of explaining to do.* "You found Eunice in one of the hotel rooms, didn't you?"

CHAPTER ELEVEN

"How do you know?" Suspicion blazing in his brown eyes, Officer Perez stared at her as though she'd committed some sort of crime.

"I don't." Yvette was quick to set the record straight. "But last night she hooked up with someone—"

"With whom?" Very interested, Sergeant Kirkpatrick leaned forward.

"I don't know his name." She felt a pang of regret for not having checked up on that fellow more closely. What if he had something to do with Eunice's death?

"Can you at least describe him?" Officer Perez snorted contemptuously.

"I only saw him for five minutes or so." On the defensive, Yvette quit playing with her phone and laid it back down on the table. "Always at a distance," she retorted more aggressively than she'd intended. Well knowing that attitude wouldn't help Eunice any, she added contritely, "I'm sorry I can't be of more help."

"It'll be enough if you tell us what happened." More understanding, Regina came to her aid. "Try to describe him as best you can."

"All right." Yvette concentrated on getting her facts in order. "As I said, we got in at around eleven-thirty. After we showed our invitations at the door—"

"By the way, how did you get those invitations?" Evidently determined to make a nuisance of himself, Carlos glared at her in an open challenge.

He could just screw himself!

She had nothing to hide, though explaining that it had been a gift after a particularly intensive sex spree might be a little tricky.

"My boss gave me three invitations." She worked hard to make it sound all sweet and innocent. "As a reward for my skillful assistance."

More for being the type of slave he'd always been searching for, but the arrogant officer didn't need the details.

"You have an outstanding boss," he remarked tartly.

"I'm an outstanding secretary." She ventured, thoroughly fed up with his tactics and uncaring about the consequences of her audacity.

"All right, so Mister Spencer gave you the invitations," Regina intervened hastily, as though she wanted to move away from this subject. "What did you do after you got there?"

"Palomar and I went to get drinks," Yvette resumed her narrative. "There was a counter at the end of the main chamber, so we joined the line of people waiting for their turn."

"Where was Eunice?" Detective Kirkpatrick inquired.

"She was . . . hem . . ." Yvette took a deep breath. "She had some problem getting through the door. You see, she was dressed as Queen Elizabeth the First, not the Second. Her costume was a bit bulky and couldn't get easily through the door."

"Figures," Carlos sneered, unsympathetically.

"Pardon?" Yvette was getting tired of his arrogant presumptions.

"I was saying that her bulk wasn't just in her dress." Defiant, the asshole glowered at her.

"Officer, why do I sense some hostility here?" Yvette didn't allow him to stare her down. "Does the NOPD have some issue with fat people?"

"The NOPD has no such issue," Detective Kirkpatrick

declared firmly, eyeballing Officer Perez until he had to avert his gaze. "Now, please, let's continue."

"Yes, ma'am." Feeling elated as if she'd won a battle of sorts, Yvette was more than happy to pick up from where she'd been rudely interrupted by the jackass. "When Eunice joined us, we had practically reached the counter, so I ordered for the three of us."

"What did you have?" Detective Kirkpatrick seemed genuinely interested.

"Long Island Iced Tea," Yvette supplied. "One of my favorites."

"It's also one of mine." Regina winked a bit conspiratorially. "Eunice had it, too?"

"We all had the same," Yvette confirmed. "The bartender handed her the first drink, but as she was moving out of the line, she bumped against this man and spilled her drink all over him."

From Officer Perez's snort, Yvette imagined he would've mumbled another, "Figures," had he only been free to do so.

Fortunately for Yvette, he wasn't.

"It was an accident, of course." She was quick to defend her friend from this new unspoken accusation. "Eunice has never been clumsy or anything."

Quite the opposite, in fact. Eunice had a grace all her own that Yvette had sometimes envied.

"Yeah, sure." This time, the bastard officer had lost a fabulous opportunity to keep his damn trap shut.

"I'm sure it was," Detective Kirkpatrick cut him off. "Was that how she met the man?"

"Yeah." Avoiding the dickhead's gawk, Yvette fixed her focus on the sergeant. "It was."

"Now, can you give us a description of this man?" Regina prompted with an encouraging smile.

"As I said, I didn't get the chance to look at him too

closely." Taking a deep breath, Yvette tried recreating a mental picture of him. "He was Caucasian, tall, very tall like . . ." Tony Spencer flashed in her mind, and she realized that man had been taller. "Six feet five if not six. He was lean and muscular and seemed tanned like someone who spends a lot of time outdoors." Where she'd picked up this detail, she didn't know, but something about the man had made her think of farms and horses. "Like he worked in a stable or something."

"Age?" Regina pressed.

"Late forties, early fifties." She recalled the comment about the guy not being a day older than fifty. "Maybe more early fifties," she corrected. "He was wearing a Count Dracula costume, so that's how we referred to him."

"You got to speak to Eunice about him?" From her surprise, it was apparent Regina hadn't expected it.

"Yes, we did for about five minutes," Yvette replied. "After such a mess, Eunice and the guy moved to a corner to assess the damage, I suppose." She smiled at her pun. "While Palomar and I finished waiting for our drinks, the man returned to the line for the counter, so Palomar and I joined Eunice. We talked a bit while he was busy getting her a new drink."

"What did you talk about?" Regina shifted on her chair.

"Oh, it was nothing important." Remembering the banter they had exchanged made it feel so trite. "We complimented her on having hooked up with someone in such a short time." Yvette felt sad that the last thing she'd shared with Eunice had been so stupid. "We also made plans on how we were to get back home. That's when we decided to split at two, but if any of us had something better to do, she'd send a text."

"Did Eunice send you such a text?" Detective Kirkpatrick's intelligent gaze bore into hers.

"No, neither Palomar nor I received any text from her after last night." How she wished now that Eunice had sent a sign. "We looked for her everywhere when it was time to leave but couldn't find her. We sent her a text telling her that we were going home, but she never replied. That's why, this morning, we were worried about her." Fresh tears stung behind her eyelids. "She's the sort of person who always answers, even if it's just to say okay, and she never misses work. Never. In all the time I've known her, she never skipped a day, not even if she was sick."

"I see." After checking on the notes Officer Perez had been taking, Detective Kirkpatrick switched her focus back on her, seemingly studying her face intently. "Would you give us permission to look through your texts?" She stretched her arm forward to take Yvette's cell.

"Now?" Instinctively, her hand wrapped around the Note Twenty she'd bought two days ago.

"Yes, now, if you don't mind," Detective Kirkpatrick urged.

"I don't understand." It was one thing to cooperate with the police, quite another to lay bare all the secrets concealed in her very active text-life. "If Eunice died of natural causes, why all the questions? Why do you need to verify every-thing?"

"Even if there's nothing suspicious about your friend's death at present, the circumstances in which she was found are a bit odd," Regina explained with a surprisingly patient tone. "She was found in a hotel room, not her house, and that's enough for us to have to require an autopsy and inves-tigate the matter."

"An autopsy?" My God, she hadn't even thought about it. "I didn't realize . . ." Yvette's voice trailed off in embarrassed silence.

"Most people don't, Miss Carlisle." Detective Kirkpatrick beamed at her as though in complete solidarity. "That's why we ask for your understanding and cooperation in verifying your statements as much as possible."

Am I a suspect? Since this was the kind of question culprits always asked in the TV crime series she loved, Yvette kept her peace. Instead, she picked up the phone, pressed her fingertip to slide open the lock screen, and pushed it toward Regina. "You have my permission to look through my texts."

"Thanks, Miss Carlisle." Eagerly grabbing the black device, Regina huddled closer to Carlos and quickly got busy, sliding open windows and apps while her partner watched.

Yvette wondered what they'd make of the triple-X texts Tony sent daily as reminders of who was in charge. Good thing she'd saved his private number only as Sortilege M and not under his real name. Then again, she didn't give a crap what the two police officers would think of her. Her life was her own business, and since it broke no law, she was entitled to it.

After a couple of minutes, Regina handed back her phone. "Thanks, we appreciate it."

"If there's anything else I can do." Tentatively, Yvette glanced at her watch and realized she'd been cooped up here for nearly an hour.

Carlos Perez was quick to take advantage of her offer. "Yes, you could direct us to Miss Redondo."

"To Palomar?" Evidently, NOPD was thorough and didn't want to leave any stones unturned. "Sure, if she hasn't gone to lunch." Relieved to be off the hook, she picked up her Note Twenty and rose. "I'll go call her."

"Officer Perez will accompany you," Detective Kirkpatrick offered immediately.

That information made Yvette suspect that they didn't want her to give Palomar any sneak previews.

"All right," she conceded, none too happy, but then this was their game and their rules. "Let's go." Uncaring of the idiot's whereabouts, she went to the door, opened it, and crossed the hallway.

Chapter Twelve

"Have you heard back from the police?" Sipping her Margarita, Palomar raised her head to catch Yvette's gaze.

Months had passed since Eunice's death. Christmas had come and gone, and now they were at the beginning of a new year.

The funeral was also a thing of the past. Yvette couldn't remember attending a sadder affair. It had been her, Palomar, and the two surviving Saint Jacques—Javier and Francine. Two sorrier individuals than Eunice's parents couldn't be found, not even if one tried her damn best. They had sat through the brief service, impassible and unmoving as if it weren't their daughter that they were burying. She and Palomar had shed all the tears they hadn't and said all the good-byes those two had seemed unable to utter.

No wonder Eunice had fled from them as soon as she'd managed to and never looked back.

Yvette could totally sympathize.

"Nah, haven't heard anything from them." She sipped her own Margarita. "Not after that grueling interview."

"Yeah, tell me about it." Palomar nodded emphatically. "I thought I was going to die." She glanced around the posh pub they had chosen for tonight's get together. "That jerk of an officer . . ." Her lovely forehead creased. "I forget his name."

"Officer Asshole Perez," Yvette was happy to supply.

"Yeah, him," Palomar confirmed. "He was such a creep about Eunice and her weight."

"All his implying that she couldn't lead a normal life or be happy simply because she was fat," Yvette snorted disgust-edly.

"With me, he was about to ask me how I could be friends with someone like her," Palomar remarked indignantly.

Point of fact, neither she nor Palomar had ever seen Eunice as a fat person. They hadn't befriended her because they felt sorry for her. Absolutely not! They had both seen her as a fragile woman who had needed friends to get out of her shell. That was what she'd most craved even if unconsciously, and Yvette was mighty glad that she'd succeeded.

However short their acquaintance, she and Palomar had made a difference in Eunice's life, and it was Yvette's best damn achievement to date.

"These are the kind of people who pass judgment on others without even knowing who they really are." Yvette shook her head.

Palomar set the record straight once and for all. "Those people are called racist and prejudiced."

"The worst part is that he was of the NOPD," Yvette re-torted. "Which is fucking scary."

"Those kinds of creeps are everywhere." Palomar slurped down the last of her drink. "Not just in the NOPD."

"Well, ours was in the NOPD." Remembering him made her queasy. "He was making so many smart-ass cracks about her that the detective had to restrain him." The image of Re-gina Kirkpatrick's eloquent put-down-stare made her feel im-mediately better. "Imagine that!"

"Yeah, you told me," Palomar reminded.

"I was just glad to see both of them go," she added. "I really didn't like all their questions or the way they looked at you as though you were a suspect."

"All for nothing." Yvette sighed.

The autopsy had concluded that it had been heart failure, after all. No cuts, no shots, no bruises, no vampire bites, no strange marks anywhere, so there had been no foul play. Those officers had packed away their notes and left after having talked to her and Palomar alone, satisfied that everything had checked out in the end.

Yvette wasn't as convinced.

Something about Eunice's death still bugged her as though it wasn't natural. As though someone had killed her.

Which was absurd given the evidence.

Yvette sighed. "I wonder what happened to him."

"Who?" Holding her empty glass, Palomar flagged down the waiter.

"Count Dracula." Yvette finished her cocktail in time to order a refill. "Remember him?"

"Hem . . ." Palomar's gaze remained glued to the waiter's firm ass. "Sure." With an effort, her friend's focus shifted on Yvette. "Hard to forget."

Not a lie.

Yvette had wondered more than once about him. What had really happened the night Eunice had died? Why hadn't the police been able to trace him anywhere?

"I tried looking for him," she confessed as soon as the waiter had left their new drinks.

"You did?" Palomar was again eyeballing the attractive backside of the man who was now going to another customer.

Looking over her shoulder, Yvette had to admit that the sight was worthwhile.

"Why?" After sipping the frosty-looking Margarita. Palomar set it down on the table. "What do you need to know from him?"

"What happened to Eunice that night." The cold drink slipped down her throat and burned her stomach. "I mean, don't you think that her death was kind of strange?"

"Come on, Yve." Palomar stared at her agape. "Don't tell me you still believe she didn't have a heart attack?"

"No, she did." There could be no way to doubt it, given the autopsy report. "But something must've caused it, don't you think?"

"You think that guy had something to do with it."

Palomar's statement summed up Yvette's suspicions quite nicely. "Yeah." She nodded in confirmation. "You see, I don't buy it. Eunice was healthy, plus she was too young to have heart problems."

"The police thought that her weight made heart failure a plausible cause of death," Palomar recalled.

"Ha! The police!" Yvette scoffed. "To Officer Asshole Perez, Eunice was just another fatso who got what she deserved!"

"Yve, why are you getting angry?" Palomar grabbed her hand and clasped it forcefully. "What's going on?"

"Sorry." Yvette squeezed back. "I didn't mean to snap, but it doesn't seem right about Eunice dying that way."

"I know, chica," Palomar cooed softly. "It doesn't seem fair that she should go so young."

"I miss her, Palomar." Holding on to her friend, she felt the sting behind her eyelids and wished she could cry, wished that whatever tears she might shed could take away the dull emptiness that devoured her more every day.

"Me, too." There was nothing except sincere sadness in Palomar's voice. "At work, it's the hardest. Every day, I expect her to be there—"

"When I see her empty place, I only wanna leave," Yvette agreed.

"Yeah." Letting go of her hand, Palomar drank a generous swallow. "It hurts to see that empty office of hers."

Goldblum had never gotten around to replacing Eunice. Rather than hire someone new, they had outsourced the whole accounting department to a prominent firm.

"You shouldn't let it get to you like this." Now worried,

Palomar's tone became stern, "She's gone, and there's nothing you can do about it."

Except hunting down her killer. Since this kind of talk would make Palomar think her crazy, Yvette kept it to herself. "Maybe, Count Dracula could shed new light on this," she offered instead.

"Or maybe not." Palomar contradicted in a sensible tone that made Yvette want to cry all over again. "Either way, if the police didn't track him down, how could you?"

"I don't think they ever looked for him. I mean, how hard could it have been to figure out who he was? He must've been on the party's guest list, and he must've checked in when he'd gotten a room at La Maison del Fuego, don't you think?"

"Yeah, probably." Palomar sounded doubtful. "Since they didn't bother checking him out, how could you do it now after three months?"

"I have no idea," Yvette grunted. "I keep hoping I meet him somewhere."

"Maybe, he'll show up at Club Sortilege." Palomar giggled.

"That'll be the day," Yvette joined in, relaxing a bit. "I don't see him as a Dom or a Master."

"I don't see him, period," Palomar was quick to point out. "We never really had the chance to look at him properly." She took another swig from her cocktail. "The chamber was kind of dark with all that candlelight."

"I think I'd recognize him if I saw him."

"Even at the club?" Palomar insisted. "Even if masked?"

Of course, it was a wisecrack. Palomar had nothing to do with Club Sortilege and its hot BDSM scene. That was Yvette's domain.

Palomar was more traditional. She wanted a man to love and cherish her, a man to settle down with, marry, and have beautiful children together. That the woman had been actively looking for Mister Right without much success hadn't deterred her from believing he was out there somewhere and that one day she'd magically find him. Still, Palomar was open-minded enough to accept Yvette's alternative lifestyle without the slightest judgment or criticism, and it was the reason they were so close.

"I'd recognize him from his dick," Yvette bragged jokingly.

"Don't tell me you've memorized them all." Palomar laughed out loud.

"No, but he'd be a new dick." Yvette snickered, trying to rationalize it no matter how absurd she sounded. "One I had never seen, so I'd identify him pronto."

"How many cocks have you seen exactly?" Palomar's beautiful black eyes widened.

Hundreds for sure. "Oh, I haven't counted them all." She downplayed it on purpose. "The cock itself isn't all that exciting. It's the man wielding it that makes all the difference."

"Yeah, tell me about it." Reaching for the bowl of peanuts she'd hardly touched, Palomar took a few and munched on them. "I've had some pretty hot guys with a wonderful dick whose performance was a total disaster."

Yvette took the first sip of her new Margarita. "That's why Tony Spencer is such a master."

Not something she would advertise at the office, of course. Palomar and Eunice had been the only ones to know about their affair and sat through the endless retelling of his most torrid acts.

"I seriously think you're in love with the guy," Palomar stated in challenge. "So did Eunice."

Nothing new here. This light banter was always part of Yvette's discussions with Palomar and Eunice, and she'd come to love it.

"You gals are so old-fashioned," she taunted dismissively. "Like I told you, I'm in it for the sex alone."

Palomar sniggered. "Is that why you're wearing his

collar."

Yvette rolled her eyes. "The collar doesn't mean anything, and you know it." She fingered the slim, white-gold metal around her neck. "It's merely an exciting reminder that I belong to someone else even if I'm free to screw whoever I like." She elaborated even though there was no need for it. "It turns every master who lays hands on me the hell on."

"I still don't get it," Palomar pressed. "I mean, you're a slave, right?"

"Technically, yes," Yvette acknowledged. "But I'm not a one-master type of slave. I'm what you'd call a submissive who needs many Doms to keep her satisfied."

"Tony accepts it?" Despite her skeptical tone, Palomar knew he did since they had talked about it often enough.

"He's the first one to be turned on by it." Yvette dipped into the peanut bowl. "He's also the first one who has understood that one cock just doesn't cut it with me." She nibbled on her peanuts. "You should see him when we're in a threesome or foursome."

The way Tony offered her to those other men made her wet all over. His choice of men, naturally, never hers since she had no rights in that department. Then, he would take complete charge of the scene, and she risked dying from sheer pleasure. Commanding the others, he would tell them what holes to fill and how. He'd decide when they had rammed her enough–when her ass was as large as her pussy–for his colossal monster to take her without any sweat. Such was usually his goal whenever he invited other masters to his game.

"I can't even imagine." Palomar shook her head, amused. "Most women I know have enough of a hard time simply to find the right guy while you juggle multiple partners at once."

"I'm not most women," Yvette retorted.

"That's for sure." There was a definite note of admiration in Palomar's tone. "I don't know how you do it."

"It's easy if you think it's just sex." She sipped her cocktail. "Besides, Tony isn't my master alone. He's got lots of subs and slaves drooling over him at the club, who'd give their right arm for a fraction of his attention."

"Me, I'd get jealous as hell," Palomar recognized ruefully.

"I'm not." Yvette was quick to clear the air. "He can have as many women or men as he likes, as long as I can have the same freedom he has."

"Yeah, sure." Palomar scoffed. "What if he asked you to stop screwing around? Or worse, what if he found a younger, more obedient sub to enslave and send you packing?" She regarded Yvette as though she was up against a corner. "What would you do then?"

CHAPTER THIRTEEN

"I'd find a new master," had been Yvette's instinctive response to Palomar's last question.

Now, watching Tony's powerful, very muscular body advancing toward a petite blonde, a new arrival at Club Sortilege, she wasn't so sure.

Something about Tony Spencer bewitched her. Maybe, it was the effortless way he took control of any situation, whether at work or at the club. Maybe, it was his impressive frame and the ease with which he commanded everyone—men and women alike. Whatever it was, it had hooked her good and proper, and perhaps Palomar had been voicing a real concern.

Had his enslavement gone beyond the sex?

"Mistresses and Masters, welcome to Presentation Night," Tony's deep masculine voice boomed in the main chamber and snapped Yvette out of her reveries.

Standing in a circle of slaves behind the ring of masters and mistresses, she glanced at the torches burning on the walls of a cave-like dungeon. Visibility wasn't a priority, but her eyes had soon adjusted to the dimmer hue.

"Also known as Slave Initiation Night," Tony added in a huskier tone.

The name said it all. Whoever wanted to become a slave in New Orleans would have to start here.

There always were so many of them that the club filled on these nights. Usually, though, only a very few passed the rigorous selection. Then again, only a very few were true submissive. Most of the applicants didn't have what it took to be a real slave, even if they thought otherwise.

This night typically dispelled their illusions.

"Tonight, we'll choose three—no more than three—to become Club Sortilege's slaves of the month." Even if everyone already knew the rules, Tony spelled them out anyway. "These individuals have forfeited their consent, and the chosen ones will become the exclusive property of Club Sortilege." His firm gaze swept the chamber. "Of course, I don't need to remind anyone that it's an honor and a privilege to serve all of Club Sortilege's many patrons."

Something akin to a wave of excitement seemed to emanate from the cluster of potential subs. How to blame them?

If picked, the new slaves would have to remain within the club for the entire month, not allowed to go anywhere except in the private rooms. They would eat, sleep, and live at the club for the whole month. In short, they wouldn't have a life besides their sexual one.

Yvette remembered with pleasure when she'd been among the chosen ones. Tony had told her to apply, and she had against her reservations. Knowing the Grand Master hadn't made her selection process any easier. If anything, it had been more grueling than most, for he'd been particularly brutal with her. She'd passed anyway and spent a glorious month on her back, gaining invaluable training that made up for all the servitude she had to endure.

"The pool of contenders is over there." Tony gestured at a large locked cage on the far side. "We can start now." Taking a step back, he settled so that he was out of the way yet surveyed the entire place. "Doms may approach the slave's pen."

Masters and mistresses wore masks for this special occasion. It was the distinguishing feature, the thing that set them apart from ordinary mortals. Yvette had often wondered why the club would go to such lengths since clothing already defined everyone's role. As a slave, for instance, she was required to be scantily clad in leather strings that left breasts, vagina, and ass exposed. Totally unlike the Doms, who wore whatever they fancied and covered their strategic parts.

Besides, since this mask thing hid their identity most effectively, Presentation Night brought many new Doms to Club Sortilege. Tonight, quite a few of them were strangers to her.

They were clustering near the cage, walking around its outer perimeter, and studying what was on offer.

From her place, Yvette couldn't see the display, and she had to wait her turn. Although slaves didn't participate in the selection process, they were allowed to peek at the contenders and make suggestions if anybody important bothered to ask them.

When Tony signaled it, she proceeded toward the enclosure. Tonight, it was crowded. Naked young men and women made their best effort at appearing submissive. Most failed.

Looking up eagerly at every master or mistress passing by, they proved how little they had acquired of a sub's etiquette. The few notable exceptions kept their gazes downcast, betraying neither excitement nor anticipation. It wasn't a slave's place to show such emotions, after all. It was always the Dom's prerogative to command them, and so far, these poor bastards were no one's property, not even their own.

Two of those exceptions caught Yvette's eyes.

One was a tall brunette on the plump side, with a noticeable double belly and sturdy thighs. This would-be slave resembled Eunice a bit, which was why Yvette looked at her twice. The woman was undoubtedly different from all the anorexics present. Skin and bone — that was the regular appearance of female slaves as if thinness were a mark of beauty and obedience. As if it were an outfit in itself.

Even if Yvette herself was on the lean side, she never scorned the more opulent types. Like Eunice, they often had a distinctive appeal that was more subtle than the malnourished one most women cultivated with such dedication and passion.

This brunette possessed it. Yvette could tell from her stance she was entirely at ease in her body and thought it attractive enough to proffer it in slavery. The relaxed way she was examining her feet also expressed a studied indifference to the procedure, which would probably increase her chances of being among the three chosen.

The second to catch Yvette's attention was a redhead male with oval-shaped hazel eyes. If she managed to notice their color, it wasn't because he was staring upward. It was because when she strolled by him, he gave her a quick peek from under very long, very thick eyelashes.

He was shorter and younger than the brunette. Unlike the woman, he had a fair complexion with a scattering of freckles that made him look adorable and innocent. Good enough to eat was Yvette's appraisal, and she was pretty confident that others had noticed, too.

Sure enough, it was a master that she'd never seen before, stepping toward Tony. He demanded to have a closer inspection of the redhead.

Well, no surprise there, were it not that something about this particular master seemed kind of familiar.

Perplexed, Yvette moved to a corner to examine him at leisure. Had he only removed his mask, she wouldn't have had to rely on her powers of observation. She applied herself because something told her it was too important to let go.

The master in question was uncommonly tall, six feet five, or perhaps six if she had to give it a figure. He also had long black hair to the shoulders and a muscular frame without the bodybuilder's inflated mass. Something jarred her memory, but the age didn't seem to fit with the picture forming in her mind. This man seemed very young, in his late twenties or early thirties, while the one in her mind was older, *not a day older than fifty.*

Fuck!

She almost gasped out loud.

However improbable and up to verification, the master she was staring at was an excellent fit for the elusive Count Dracula of Eunice's last hours.

CHAPTER FOURTEEN

How it could be possible, Yvette had no idea.

She only knew that the more she looked at him, the more convinced she became, the more she wanted to grab his arm, drag him away, and demand an explanation.

Which, of course, was out of the question.

He was a master. She was a lowly slave. Still, she'd watch him like a hawk until she got him alone. For now, she was happy to follow the action in front of her.

Two beefy men, Club Sortilege's bodyguards, pulled the redhead out of the enclosure and flung him at Tony's feet.

"Is this the worthless piece of hide you wanted to inspect?" Tony sneered.

He was so good at demeaning people that Yvette wondered why he hadn't turned it into a profession.

"Nah." The could-be Count Dracula dismissed the claim with a wave of the hand. "He's dreadful," he snapped airily. "I wanted the other one." He pointed at the brunette still inside the pen. "The fat one."

There was nothing unusual about this whole procedure. Humiliation was a big part of Presentation Night, something the would-be slaves better get used to if they were bent on following this lifestyle.

"All right." Unruffled, Tony signaled the bodyguards. "Throw him in the unwanted corner."

The first rule about taking candidates out of the display cage was that they couldn't re-enter it. Once they were out, they were *out* and no turning back. If they had to be discarded, they'd be held at the opposite end, next to the entrance. Thick ropes sealed off this spot, but the absence of bars and locks made it less of a prison.

Which was worse.

Being such an open space, the slaves who ended up there were tempted to make a run of it.

Yvette had been cast into the unwanted lot during her presentation night, and she remembered how awful she'd felt about it. It had seemed like the end of the line for her. It had almost broken her spirit, and she still had nightmares about it.

Lucky for her, things had turned out differently in the end, as she hoped they would for the poor redhead whose sinking heart was visible from the extreme pallor of his beautiful face.

Yes, beautiful he indeed was, a delicate beauty heightened by those enormous hazel eyes that seemed to speak volumes about his inner turmoil.

No time to linger, the bodyguards were already dragging the brunette forward.

If the master standing next to Tony was indeed Count Dracula, Yvette had no doubt he would fall for this slave as he had for Eunice. Would he also go as far as killing her as he had Eunice?

Annoyed, Yvette shook her head.

There was no proof the man had done anything to accelerate her friend's demise. The fact she'd accused and convicted him didn't make him guilty, other than in her mind. Better stop with the attitude, at least until he got the chance to defend himself.

Meanwhile, events had progressed, and the brunette crouched in front of Tony's feet.

"What would you like this slut to do for you?" The Grand Master didn't even glance at the poor thing huddled on the floor.

"Let's see if she can lick my feet properly." The masked master snickered.

The plump brunette didn't wait to be told twice. She guzzled those feet as though her life depended on it, and that was her first big mistake.

"I didn't order you to start." Tony's icy tone broke through her furious laps.

Right after, one of the beefy men yanked up her head and blocked her.

"Obedience means that you do the things you're told *when* you're told to do them." The Grand Master elaborated further. "Not a moment sooner, not a moment after, but exactly the second you're told." It was pretty obvious he relished the lashing and the chastisement that it would bring. "Since you've failed to understand this basic principle, you'll have to learn it the hard way." He nodded toward the bodyguard, who was still holding the slave's hair. "Proceed," he ordered thickly.

Going to a far wall, the man picked up a paddle. Returning center stage, he raised the brunette's waist until she had to straighten her legs and flatten the palms of her hands on the floor, her double belly protruding in her arched position. Satisfied, he let her go and pulled back his arm, aiming for her ass.

Whack, whack, whack.

The brunette gasped at the rapid succession of three brutal hits to her left buttock.

"Slaves aren't allowed to utter a sound during their punishment." Tony's stern rebuke had the brunette clamping her mouth. "If I hear another sound from you, you're out of the competition."

To enforce his point, he took the paddle from the bodyguard and administered three powerful blows, always on the left buttock.

Needless to say, it turned purple.

"Continue." Tony returned the gear to the beefy man, who didn't hesitate to go for her right buttock.

Bam, bam, bam.

No whimper escaped the brunette, not even a breath, as far as Yvette could tell.

The bodyguard landed two more sets of sharp smacks before Tony deemed the lesson sufficient.

"Now that you've learned about the importance of timing," he taunted mercilessly. "Let's see how you can perform the simple task of licking a master's feet."

Slowly, very slowly, the brunette crouched back down on the floor. Unlike the last time, the woman didn't do anything.

Tony waited a moment longer, evidently wanting to trip her up again. When that didn't work, he gave her the command to start.

Pressing her face on the naked feet, she dedicated long, seemingly avid laps that covered the whole of it, from the toes to the ankle.

Everyone watched in rapt fascination and with palpable anticipation of how the master would react.

Yvette already knew this scenario and wasn't at all surprised when he exclaimed, "Get your filthy tongue off me!"

Again, one bodyguard wrenched the brunette's hair and held her still.

"She's disgusting," he stated flatly. "Grand Master, if you give me permission, I'd like to discipline this slave personally in the privacy of one of your rooms."

Tony's furrowed brow indicated he wasn't too happy about the request, and Yvette could understand why.

It was one thing to allow Club Sortilege's experienced and long-standing masters the privileges of being alone with someone who wasn't a slave yet, quite another to give the same leeway to a virtual stranger.

"I'll allow it," Tony granted. "But, only at the presence of two other masters and a trained slave of my choice."

The furious throb between Yvette's legs left her no doubt as to the identity of Tony's choice in the slave's department.

"If those are your terms . . ." The master Yvette had decided was Count Dracula hesitated as if debating with himself. "I accept," he conceded graciously after a moment's more consideration.

"Good." Tony nodded in approval. "I call on Master Devon and Master Sylvien to accompany our visiting master." Funny, he didn't offer a name. "As for the slave . . ." His steely gaze intercepted hers, and she melted all over the place. "You, slut." He pointed at her. "Follow them and obey their every order."

To indicate her submission, Yvette dropped to the floor and waited.

Rules forbade a slave from going around on her own once she'd been assigned to a master. Instead, she had to be dragged around by a leash.

Such became Master Devon's task. From the far wall that held all the torturing devices one might hope for, he picked up a whip, then approached her prone form until he was close enough to tie it to her collar. No need to take any other tools. All the rooms at Club Sortilege were amply equipped.

When he tugged her forward, Yvette offered no resistance.

Compliant and docile, she wallowed on all fours alongside him, matching her pace to his, stopping when he made a sign to the other two masters to follow him.

Since the brunette wasn't a full-fledged slave, she had no right to a leash. She had to be carried. Up she went, thrown over a bodyguard's shoulder like a sack of potatoes, and the small group left the chamber.

CHAPTER FIFTEEN

"Where do you want me to leave her?" Advancing to the middle of the room, the bodyguard seemed ready to throw the brunette on the floor.

"Tie her on the cross," Count Dracula ordered. "Then, gag and blindfold her."

As soon as the man complied, he bowed to each master in turn and left the room.

Neatly fastened by her wrists and ankles with a giant ball gag stuck in her mouth and her vision impaired, the brunette looked anxious.

Yvette had no problem noticing it, and of course her heart went out to her. It was a useless effort. The woman's destiny was as far away from her hands as the Sun was from Pluto.

Count Dracula wasted no time. From the vast array of tools, he selected a flogger and shifted the cross until the brunette's back was at his mercy.

Master Devon halted beyond the exit and wrenched Yvette's leash to sit in front of him. He set about watching Count Dracula. Only to make it more interesting for him, he unzipped his leather pants and pushed her head on a half-mast cock. "Suck," he commanded in a tone that admitted no denials.

As her mouth closed on the impressive piece, she heard the hissing of the whip delivering the sting of the first blows.

Swish, swish, swish.

Replicating the same pattern Tony himself had used, Count Dracula went about methodically punishing the poor woman for having done a poor job with his feet.

Standing next to Master Devon, Master Sylvien followed a bit of the action in front of him before his eyes fell on Yvette's luscious blowjob.

"Feel like sharing?" Yanking her hair, Master Devon swung her head toward Master Sylvien.

"If you don't mind," the man grumbled, dissatisfied.

"Not at all," Master Devon consented graciously. "There aren't many slaves to go around, after all."

That was a real pity and an exception to the rules. Yvette could count on the fingers of one hand the times when masters outnumbered slaves, and this was one of them.

"Right." To make his claim known, Master Sylvien forced three thick fingers down her throat until she gagged on them. "Why don't we watch the show from over there?" Removing his digits from her mouth, he indicated a spacious couch on a side. "You can have her mouth while I have fun with her ass."

The mere thought of it sent a shiver of pleasure coursing through her back.

Master Devon assented and dragged her by the hair to the intended destination.

Meanwhile, Count Dracula increased the rhythm of the blows, using sets of four or five. He was enjoying himself tremendously, judging from a cursory glance of his crotch that Yvette managed to steal.

Soon, he wouldn't be able to stand the pressure, and the slave would have more on her ass than just a flogger.

"Here." Finally letting go of her hair, Master Devon sank in the comfortable red-leather cushions. "Let's settle this slut so we can both take what we want from her."

"I have just the position in mind." Master Sylvien chuckled.

Clutching her waist, he walked behind the couch and leaned her over the back.

Figured he'd choose a place from which both masters could observe Count Dracula and his discipline lessons.

As she dangled from the edge, Master Devon pulled her head forward, shifting her enough for his dick to find its way down her throat. Or up, depending on your point of view.

Not content, Master Sylvien fetched several items from the supply table.

She was too busy on Master Devon's enormous cock to notice what they were, but she had no doubt she'd soon find out. Not surprisingly, the first was a butt plug, a huge one splitting her backside to bits from the force of Master Sylvien's penetration.

"Do you like that, bitch?"

His snarl had an undercurrent of excitement that intoxicated her more than she could've believed. "Yes, Master," she sputtered in between gulps of air.

If it wasn't precisely the truth, she didn't rush to put it to rights. The damn thing had dilated her ass ring all together and all at once. Wedged so deep inside, it was doubtful it could ever get out in one piece.

"Do you really?" Master Sylvien's new remark alerted her that maybe he'd sensed her reservations.

Before she could respond appropriately, a nasty spank on her left buttock almost had her swallowing Master Devon's demanding monster for real. Soon after, a second and a third followed, making her skin cringe. From the impacts, she guessed he must be using a leather paddle and getting so much fun out of it that even Count Dracula stopped his thrashing to watch him.

Yvette's skin felt redder with each consecutive blow delivered by this unflinching master. She'd never played with him, only heard tales of his severe punishments.

Well, this must be it!

Stoically, she braced herself for a new round, hoping the pain would soon give way to pleasure. That was how it always happened with her, and it was also the reason she'd never give up this lifestyle. If she hung on long enough, the unbearable pain switched to unimaginable bliss and allowed her to soar in ecstasy.

"Damn slut," Master Sylvien sneered. "You like this, don't you?" As though to prove it, he dipped another dildo in her pussy.

From the way she gobbled it up, she was way damper than she'd initially assessed. So much so, she came as soon as it was up to the hilt. It was an explosion of the senses. Her body convulsed frantically around both stuffings, sending wave after exquisite wave of pleasure down her toes and up her hair.

She climaxed hard. So hard, she barely noticed when Master Sylvien removed the butt plug and stuck his colossal shaft up her ass. Being as large as she was, her ass offered no impediments to his slide to her guts. He took advantage of it to ram as forcefully as he could.

On her front, Master Devon had also stepped up the tempo, fucking her face in a faster upbeat that suffocated her every time he raised his hips.

Of course, she could do nothing except take it all.

She was a slave. They were the masters.

It was as simple as that.

As arousing, too.

The feeling of being utterly dominated always managed to tip her overboard regardless of how much they abused her.

At their latest, coordinated shove in her ass and mouth, she burst.

As did they, pulling out and spraying thick ropes of sweet cum all over her face and ass.

When Yvette succeeded in averting her focus from her physical vortex, she saw that Count Dracula had untied the brunette from the cross and had placed her on the bondage bench. Stretched out and leaning on her elbows, knees bent, double belly hanging down, and ass pushed out, she made a compelling picture. The total effect was further heightened by the open-mouth-gag the masked master had fitted on her face and used to feed her a veritable beast.

Yvette almost gasped.

Even though she was used to massive rods, seldom had she seen one so vast in both girth and length. It made her mouth water at the mere sight of it, and she had to suppress a pang of envy for the lucky brunette who had no choice in eating it up to her throat or, more appropriately, being stifled without pity.

At the spectacle, Master Devon got up from the sofa and neared the pair. "Do you mind if I play with your slave?"

"Be my guest." Count Dracula gestured for him to proceed. "But I have to warn you that she isn't particularly good."

"For sure, she isn't trained." Grasping a dildo and a butt plug, Master Devon stopped at the brunette's backside. "That's what we're here for." Separating her thick thighs, he impaled her slit with an exceptionally substantial dildo that found no friction thanks to her exceedingly drenched state. "Aren't we?" He spread her ass cheeks wide apart and screwed a medium-sized butt plug in it.

Having had them both herself, Yvette would've liked to observe the woman's reactions, which wasn't on Master Sylvien's agenda.

Pushing Yvette on the couch, he hoisted her legs in the air and slammed into her derriere once more.

Good grief, when had he gotten so stiff?

He'd just unloaded all over her, yet he was as rigid as if he hadn't come at all.

Best of all, he also handled a giant size dildo that she was sure would soon replace the one still wedged in her pussy.

"Ready for a second one, slut?"

Or maybe not. It seemed this master had the insane notion that she'd prefer two to one in her vagina. She most definitely did not, though she couldn't say it.

With a mixture of horror and bewitchment, she followed his hand as it brought the dildo next to the one already occupying her front space. Using a tenderness she didn't think he possessed, his fingers created more space where none seemed to exist, then he slowly inserted the second dildo and rotated it.

Oh, boy, she was going to explode for sure.

Between the giant dick cracking her ass and the two pieces stretching her pussy, Yvette didn't think she'd make it out of that room alive.

Uncaring, he went about thrusting the second device up to her belly, hammering her backside at the same time.

To distract her body, she glanced at the other scene playing out in front of her.

The brunette was off the bench, and Master Devon was arranging her on the bed opposite the couch. On all fours, he removed the dildo and the butt plug, and not a moment too soon.

Under Yvette's captivated stare, Count Dracula sank in the woman's yielding cunt while Master Devon targeted her ass.

The brunette squirmed, a sure sign that she'd never experienced a double penetration and was liking it more than she'd imagined. Or so, Yvette interpreted the woman's attempts at adjusting her position.

She wished she could follow more of the action, but her own predicament had gotten dramatic. Having inserted the second dildo up to the hilt, Master Sylvien was driving his cock in a frenzy of orgiastic pleasure. The gig he'd set up included a severe pumping of her cunt along with her butt.

If she had thought she'd been cramped before, it had been nothing compared to the extreme confinement of her holes now. She was so tightly packed she could barely move.

That was when Master Sylvien had the bad idea of allowing his fingers to stray on her clit and rub it like there was no tomorrow.

It was the end of her. She shattered.

Literally!

Pure, unabated pleasure shot through her every fiber, and she had to bite down on her tongue not to scream her orgasm to the world.

Incredible enough, Master Sylvien was right alongside her, blasting juice on her belly and breasts while the sound of the other two masters also climaxing reached her ears.

Could anything be more perfect?

CHAPTER SIXTEEN

"Master Adrien, would you have a moment for me?" Having spotted Count Dracula at the plush lounge bar set aside exclusively for Club Sortilege's members, Yvette moved to stand in front of his booth.

"Who told you my name?" Astonishment and distrust clouded his beautiful purple eyes.

They were such an unusual shade that she had to keep herself from staring at them too closely.

"The Grand Master graciously told me who you are."

Nah, Tony's input had been anything but gracious. He'd only coughed up the information after she'd threatened to deprive him of her ass for the next fifteen days or so.

"May I sit down?" She glanced at the empty seat in front of Master Adrien.

The nice thing about Club Sortilege's Lounge Bar was there were no masters and no slaves.

People could just be themselves, dressed in their usual everyday clothes, and no one could make any demands on them. It was a free zone where members could relax and mingle with others if they so wished.

Or not mingle, depending on their mood, like Master Adrien, who looked very much like he wanted to be left alone.

"Please do." He consented after a few seconds, to her surprise and joy.

Quick to take advantage of his offer before he had the chance to change his mind, she perched on the edge of the seat and took a few moments to study him up close.

Adrien Ascott was handsome, no question about it, especially given those stunning purple eyes that seemed to contain age-old wisdom. Strange yet exciting, this man seemed to have stepped from the past with his rugged good looks, masculine face with a square jaw, high cheekbones, and aquiline nose. The only detail that jarred with everything else was his age, which couldn't have been more than late twenties like she'd surmised in the chamber.

"What is it?" He ended her scrutiny brusquely. "I don't have much time." To stress his point, he glanced at a watch on his right wrist.

"This won't take long, sir." She composed her face to become the unassuming slave. "I think we've met before."

"When?" Adrien narrowed his gaze. "Where?"

"It was at last year's Halloween party." Had she needed further proof for her suspicions, his purple eyes zooming on her raised her hackles. "The one held at the hotel La Maison del Fuego." Since he didn't light up in recognition, she elaborated. "You were dressed as Count Dracula." Examining the smooth lines of his face, she wondered if indeed it had been him. "At least, I think it was you, only today you look much younger."

"I was tired then," he clarified as if in a rush to justify himself. "I may not have looked my best."

"You did indeed look older." *Like in your fifties while now you're in your twenties.* Not worth saying, she concentrated on more practical details. "Anyway, my friend, Eunice, spilled her cocktail on you by accident. She was dressed as —"

"Queen Elizabeth, yes." The purple eyes flashed. "I remember now." Briefly, he raised his gaze as though to check who might be listening to this conversation.

No one was. The two of them were utterly alone in the deserted lounge. "You're one of her friends. Fancy meeting you here." He chuckled as if it would lessen the awkwardness of bumping into one another in a BDSM club. "How is she?"

"She's dead," Yvette stated flatly.

"Really?" Was it her impression, or was there no trace of surprise in his voice? "How did it happen?"

"She had a heart attack."

Yvette couldn't figure out why this man was so hard to read. Usually, she never had any problems sizing up people. With him, though, it felt different, like he was hiding behind a screen.

"I'm sorry." This time, his emotional response seemed genuine.

"She'd never had any problems with her heart." Yvette kept pursuing her track, even if it was apparent he wasn't in any sharing mood. "That's why I'd like to know if she was all right when you were together, or if you noticed something strange." She paused to give herself courage for her next inquiry. "Forgive my bluntness, but what did you do after you bought her a second cocktail?"

"Is this an interrogation, Miss . . ." He stared at her in an open challenge.

"I'm Yvette Carlisle," she offered. "The Grand Master's slave." She fingered her collar to give it more of an official ring.

"Is that so?" His lips curving upward, Adrien leaned back on his seat. "I was wondering why he chose you to witness my scene."

"He chose me 'cause he trusts my reports," she informed coldly. "As he always says, you can never be too careful with newcomers." Feeling tension tightening her shoulders, she forced herself to keep calm. "Which brings the question, where do you come from?"

"Oh, here, there, and everywhere."

A silliest, vaguest answer he couldn't have given had he even tried. "Like the Beatles' song?" Yvette taunted on purpose.

"Ah, you are a sly one." He grinned widely. "Can I offer you something to drink?" He looked around for a waiter. "A Long Island Iced Tea, perhaps?"

How about that?

He did remember.

"Thanks." Impressed in spite of herself, she shifted into a more comfortable position. "I'd love one."

A bartender appeared from nowhere behind the counter and hurried to their booth as soon as Master Ascott snapped his fingers.

"A Long Island Iced Tea for the lady and a Negroni for me," he ordered in a leisurely tone, indicating that all his earlier haste had disappeared. "What did you want to know about your friend?"

Yvette didn't miss a beat. "How she died."

"Do you think I had something to do with it?" It didn't sound like an accusation, yet he regarded her coldly.

"Well . . ." She thought about how to answer. Of course, she had no proof of foul play, not even if there had been any. Just her gut instinct told her something didn't feel right about Eunice's death.

Yeah, sure, but why did she believe this man might have played a part in it? In provoking heart failure?

It was ludicrous!

Then again, wasn't it common knowledge that the last one to see the victim alive was also the most likely culprit?

"No, of course not," she denied but added more briskly, "Or rather, not directly. Maybe, it was something you did together."

"Like having sex?" Adrien's eyebrows rose upward.

"Yeah, I suppose that could do it." She shrugged. "I don't know really," she was forced to confess. "It seems so incredible, and I still can't believe she's gone." She took a long breath to avoid breaking down and crying her heart out. "She was such a fantastic person, sweet, funny, learned, warmhearted, optimistic despite everything that had gone wrong in her life. I just want —"

"You just want answers." He cut her off in a strangely mellow tone.

"Yeah, I guess."

Taking a handkerchief from her purse, she wiped her eyes and blew her nose. The break coincided with the bartender bringing over snacks and drinks. She eagerly slurped down a generous swallow of hers to steady her nerves.

"Listen, I understand." He set his drink aside after his own sizeable swallow. "You're upset about your friend dying that way. What was her name again?"

"Eunice," she mumbled.

"I don't remember. I called her Elizabeth if I called her by name at all." His gaze locked on hers. "You see, we didn't get to talk much."

"You were in the chamber for a while," she contradicted. "I saw you."

"We were making jokes about who we were impersonating," he recalled. "Turns out, Eunice was kind of an expert of Tudor times."

"History was her favorite subject." She grabbed a few peanuts and munched them. "She was always telling us about one historical fact after another."

"She knew a lot about Queen Elizabeth and her time," he confirmed readily. "That's why we joked about it while we had our drinks."

"Are you an expert, too?" To wash down the salty taste, she sipped more tea.

"Not exactly." He dug into the chips. "But I like my history." He swallowed a mouthful. "It's what makes us unique."

"How so?" Intrigued, she leaned forward.

"It's obvious history has shaped mankind," he explained. "As a people, we are who we are because of everything that has happened to us during all the past centuries." He drank down another generous swallow of his Negroni. "This applies to our personal history as well, and that's what fascinates me." Putting the glass back down on the table, he studied her face intently. "How do we come to be who we are?"

CHAPTER SEVENTEEN

"How did you?" If this guy wanted to play, she was more than ready for him.

"Mine is a long story." He seemed reluctant to delve into it.

She wouldn't stand being put off. "I haven't got anything better to do." She smiled her sweetest smile, hoping to convince him to spill his guts.

"Doesn't your master need you?" He raised a quizzical eyebrow.

"Not now." She was sure of it.

Tony would be checking out the three who had made it as slaves of the month, which included both the redheaded and the brunette, she was glad to report.

"I've got all the time you need." To hide her eagerness, she took a sip of her Long Island Iced Tea.

Adrien Ascott glowered at her. It was apparent he was debating whether to go ahead or blow her off with one lie or another.

"All right." Having evidently made up his mind, he leaned forward. "I don't see the harm in telling you a bit about myself." He finished his Negroni. "Let me order another round before we get down to it." Holding up his empty glass, he caught the bartender's attention. "Would you like another one?" He pointed at her half-empty drink.

"Yeah, thanks." Hastily, she gulped down the rest of her cocktail and put away the tall glass.

"I'm French," he began. "I come from Aix-en-Provence. Do

you know where that is?"

She shook her head. Geography wasn't her strong suit!

"It's in the French Riviera," he explained. "Also known as Côte d'Azur."

"I know what that is." Yes, she'd heard of this renowned vacation spot. "The ones who've been there say it's beautiful."

"It is." From the dreamy note in his voice, she suspected he missed it. "There's nothing quite like it in the world."

The bartender approached, and Adrien made room for him, setting the empty glasses aside. After placing the new drinks at the center of the table, the bartender picked up the empty ones and left.

"When I was young, I worked as a stable hand at Le Clerque's estate." He tasted his fresh cocktail. "You probably never heard of them, but they were one of the richest and mightiest families of the region."

"I take it your family wasn't all that rich and powerful," she teased.

"Not when I was born," he admitted regretfully. "The Ascott's had been a force to reckon with up until the French Revolution." He made a face as though he still had an ax to grind against one of the most famous rebellions of all time.

Or infamous, depending on your point of view.

"The last surviving member of the family managed to escape with his head barely on his neck."

No doubt about it, he sounded bitter about the whole thing. "I suppose he managed to keep his head but lost everything else," she commented. It wasn't too much of a stretch.

"That's right," he confirmed. "Then, he rebuilt the family, but it was never the same again."

She tried connecting the dots he'd supplied so far, though they were few and wide apart. "You had a good name, but no money."

"That was basically it." A sad smile twisted his full lips.

"While the Le Clerque had it all," she concluded.

"They did." He took a deep breath. "Oh, yeah, they did." Lost in memory lane for a moment, he fixed his gaze on an invisible point in midair. "Especially the money and the stately mansions." Shaking his head free of whatever reverie had trapped it, he pursed his lips. "I was nothing to them, of course, except a lowly stable hand who took care of their precious horses."

"Sounds like you resented your position." Never one to keep things to herself, she had no scruples in speaking her mind. "Just a tiny bit," she added, amused.

"That's an understatement." He laughed out loud. "I hated them, their money, their horses, and everything else about them."

The premise wasn't bad. Yvette half-expected him to confess at having massacred the whole family in one furious sweep. If not that, she was sure he'd gotten his revenge somehow.

"My family needed the work, so I kept my head down, my mouth shut, and worked like a dog until . . ." His pause was a strategic one, meant to whet her appetite for sure.

"Until what?" Impatiently, she tossed back a long strand of hair.

"Until I met their most precious belonging." His grin had all the wickedness she would've associated with Satan himself. "Their daughter, Julia."

Aha! She could clearly see the treacherous path where this story was going.

"Julia Le Clerque was a little girl when I first met her." He gulped down more of his cocktail. "No more than ten or twelve. She seldom came to the stables, and she was always overprotected by her older brother, Marcel, and the rest of the family."

Did you rape her, then dump her body? She couldn't help

herself, though she had the good sense to avoid saying it out loud.

"I didn't much care for her." His purple gaze enlarging gave her the impression he'd somehow managed to pick up her unspoken question. "She was mostly away at a boarding school. I didn't get to see her too often."

Liar! I bet you were already plotting her downfall! "How old were you?" Yvette asked instead.

"I was . . ." His brow furrowed in concentration. "Hem . . . sixteen when I was hired." His expression relaxed. "When I saw Julia again, she was eighteen, and I was twenty-one."

She wondered whether he would now embark on a sad story of star-crossed lovers, of two love-struck beings that social standing and financial disparity had kept apart or led into tragedy.

"She'd turned into a beautiful woman." Digging for some peanuts, he stopped and peered at her. "In a way, she resembled your friend."

"Eunice?" Taken aback, her mouth fell open. "Really?"

"Yeah, she was kind of chubby with brown hair and eyes." He seemed to be reconstructing a mental picture of this Julia. "She was also already betrothed to a Count or a Marquis. I forget which."

"I bet something went wrong." She leaped straight to the conclusion. "That wedding never took place."

"Something did go wrong, but I swear it wasn't my fault." Naturally, he would rush to defend himself, even if no one had accused him yet. "I mean, I wasn't planning any mischief, honest."

"Didn't you tell me you weren't too happy about having to work for the Le Clerque?" Yvette was quick to catch his inconsistency.

"That was before. When I was sixteen." He dismissed her allegation with a wave of the hand. "At twenty-one, I was pretty much resigned to my fate and wasn't looking for any trouble."

"Was Julia?" Given the man's looks, she could easily imagine how a young, impressionable girl might fall for his type, particularly if she'd been locked up in a boarding school for most of her life.

"I suppose she was." He sighed. "She kept coming round to the stables with one excuse after another until she confessed that she'd fallen in love with me."

"And you?" Taking a much-needed sip from her second Iced Tea, she assessed him. "Were you in love with her?"

"No, I never was." There was no trace of emotion in his voice like there had been none when he'd learned that Eunice was dead.

"Did you tell her?" A new scenario took shape in her mind, one more horrible than all the ones she'd conjured up before.

"Well . . ." He hesitated. "Not in so many words."

Prick! "You mean, you let her believe —"

"She did it all by herself." He cut her off quickly.

Too quickly for her taste.

"She believed we were in love and that we should elope." He shrugged as though he had nothing to do with her fantasy. "I tried telling her it wouldn't work, but she wouldn't listen. I let her go ahead with her foolish plans, and we set up a meeting that I knew I wouldn't keep. When she realized I wouldn't come, I knew she'd return home and would continue with her life as if nothing had happened. She'd kept this affair secret, after all, fearing that her family would disapprove and intervene to break it off."

"You were hoping that once Julia realized you had no intention of eloping with her, she'd marry her Count or Marquis and live happily ever after?" It was so ludicrous she was sure he'd believed it would work.

"Yeah, something like that." He beamed at her

understanding.

God! Men were such fools. "I bet it didn't go down like you thought." It was the gentlest thing she could think of to say quickly.

"Not at all." He heaved. "It went horribly bad, actually," he admitted wryly. "She returned home, all right, but she was so upset she killed herself."

CHAPTER EIGHTEEN

"What?" Taken aback by the violence of Adrien's words, Yvette half-gasped.

"Yes, you heard right," he confirmed. "Julia killed herself, hung herself from a tree."

"I thought she'd be miserable and would do something foolish." Shocked, Yvette took a generous swallow of her cocktail. "Not that she'd pull the plug on life."

"I had no idea, either." Kind of apparent, this ignorance had weighed down on him for the stars only knew how long. "It all happened so fast. I was a bit slow in reacting."

Clasping his glass, he squeezed it tight. "Or I might've stopped her." Letting it go, he fixed the red liquid as though in a trance. "Saved her life or something." He rubbed his eyes. "Instead, I just stared at her when she came at me with all sorts of accusations, then let her storm off without doing anything except going back to work."

"What sort of accusations?" Yvette shifted in a more comfortable position.

"She shouted that I had never loved her," he supplied. "That I only used her. That I was a monster worse than any that would walk the earth that night."

"Pardon?" Maybe, she'd misheard the last bit.

"Oh, sorry." He regarded her apologetically. "I should've told you that this all happened on Halloween."

"Really?" It sounded like too much of a coincidence to be just a coincidence, something she didn't believe in, given how strongly she felt about fate and destiny. "How interesting."

Her mind spun, calculating all the probabilities. "I mean, it's not often you meet a guy who has lost two lovers on Halloween."

"I've always been unlucky on Halloween," he mused softly. "Maybe because it's also my birthday."

"Is it?" My, my, more coincidences, and they were piling up fast.

"Is that another black mark for me?" Adrien chortled, amused.

"No, but it does seem odd that everything happens to you on Halloween!" Yvette exclaimed.

"I wouldn't say *everything*," he retorted cautiously.

"I'd say that Julia and Eunice's death qualify as *everything*." *What if, instead of chance occurrences, this guy was a serial killer?*

"You're overreacting." He chastised her. "I wasn't trying to harm either of them." This statement didn't quite ring true. "I was only trying—"

"To be a son of a bitch?" Yvette had to set the record straight.

"You don't exactly mince words, do you?" Slightly offended, he glared at her. "Does your master sanction this kind of behavior?"

"Hem . . ." Suddenly aware that she was in Club Sortilege's lounge, she lowered her gaze. "Not really."

"I didn't think so," he countered. "I'll be sure to tell him to discipline you for your disrespect."

Ouch! That'll probably hurt. "Sorry, I didn't mean to offend you." She tried to look contrite. "I got carried away."

"There's no excuse for this type of insolence." He scoffed. "Julia was the same in the end, screaming stuff like a raving lunatic, like she wanted something or someone to punish me for God knows what."

"Sounds like she cursed you." This was the juiciest piece of information so far.

"That's ridiculous!" He shook his head vigorously. "I can't

start believing in absurdities just because things haven't been right since her death."

"What sort of things?" Intrigued despite her better judgment, she tried to sound nonchalant while keeping her nosiness down to a minimum.

"This and that." His wariness spoke volumes about his distrust in people. "Which have nothing to do with Julia." He drew back to the far side of the booth as though he didn't want her to pursue this track. "Heck! I haven't thought about her for years 'cause she isn't all that important."

"Doesn't sound so from the way you're talking about her," Yvette contradicted.

"She was a crazy bitch," he jeered disdainfully. "She didn't just love me. She had the insane notion that I was her fucking soul mate or whatever the hell people call their one true love." He sneered contemptuously. "Since I didn't reciprocate, the silly cow became hysterical and ran off to die."

"You don't believe in soul mates?" Yvette provoked.

"Of course not!" Adrien retorted. "There's no such thing."

She would've begged to differ. Although she hadn't met hers, she was sure there was a being out there who was made especially for her, who had the exact specifications Plato described in his writings. If having sex with multiple persons seemed like a paradox to conventional thinkers, she neither cared nor bothered to explain. She stuck to her view and the hell with everyone else.

Deciding it wasn't her place to challenge his beliefs, she moved to another track. "I suppose you also never fell in love."

"What's that got to do with anything?" He creased his forehead as though in an attempt to understand. "Need I remind you of how alternative our lifestyle is?" He chuckled. "Or are you under the impression that the Grand Master loves you?"

"I wouldn't care if he does," she argued on the defensive.

"The point isn't to find love, but to know if it exists at all, regardless of the lifestyle."

"I don't believe much in love." Clutching his glass, he spun it around a few times. "It's overrated if you ask me, and too many people think it's the cure for everything wrong in their lives."

"While everything's perfect in yours?" Yvette taunted lightly.

"I'm not saying it is," he shot back. "But for sure, love isn't the cure."

"Then, what is?" Feeling close to a revelation, she stretched forward expectantly.

"How should I know?" Adrien huffed. "You seem such an expert in the matter, you tell me."

It was a dare pure and simple.

"I will." She nearly jumped in her haste to pick up the gauntlet. "I'll start by assuming that Julia had cursed you *for real*." She emphasized the last words for his benefit. "That she'd put a spell on you —"

"Like a sortilege?" Adrien laughed at his pun.

"Yeah, you could call it that." She giggled, looking around the place before returning her gaze squarely on him. "A voodoo that has messed up your life and keeps repeating over and over."

Like killing poor innocent girls on Halloween?

"I'm talking hypothetically, of course," she threw in to encourage him to spill his guts.

"If it's to humor you, I presume there's no harm in a little guesswork." He took another swig from his drink. "Let's see . . ." His brow furrowed as though he were deep in memory lane. "Now that I think of it . . ." His expression darkened. "My life has been kind of on hold since Julia's death." He toyed with his glass, swirling the red liquid in tight circles. "Like everything stopped on that day, and I quit growing or something."

"Did you now?" Aha, something she could sink her teeth in finally. She knew all about karma and its disastrous upheavals. Like if one hadn't been good in a previous lifetime, one would face the same experience until somehow the lesson was learned.

No, worse, there'd be no budging from that point until that damn lesson had been hammered in your conscience and become a part of you. In other words, until enlightenment struck. Yvette believed it because she had to grapple with her share of lessons, but that was another story entirely.

"This definitely qualifies as a pattern, and it isn't a good one." Not by a long shot if considering Eunice's premature passing. "To get your life back, you'd have to change something." She had to drink because her throat was getting drier at every word. "Or come up with a different way of doing things."

"Are you suggesting I take Julia's rants seriously?" His eyes widened in disbelief. "Perhaps, all I have to do to set things right again is find that soul mate she was so fond of." He spat maliciously. "Miss Carlisle, do you seriously think that this curse is some sort of treasure hunt?" He regarded her with skepticism stamped all over his beautiful face. "With the prize being the soul mate?" He smiled in a veritable insulting fashion. "Maybe, just for the hell of it, she also wants me to fall in love with it if such a thing exists." He snickered though the laugh was on him.

"It does seem better than the alternative," she remarked tartly.

"Which is?" He tossed back his shoulders as though getting ready for a fight.

"That you pick up girls on Halloween." Slowly, the fog was clearing, and she was beginning to see some light at the end of the tunnel. "Who'll then die on you."

"Once!" Adrien rushed to block her. "It happened just once," he stated vehemently.

Once too many was her sad conclusion. "Poor Eunice had to pay for whatever bad mojo is going on between you and this Julia chic."

"I thought we were speaking hypothetically." His stunning purple gaze bore into hers.

"We are." Unwilling to have him catch her lie, she averted her focus. "But things don't seem to add up."

"They aren't supposed to." After draining the last drop of Negroni, he set aside the glass and glanced at her half-empty cocktail. "Do you want another?"

"Nah, I'm good." She drank down a sip.

"Look, there's nothing strange about me or the situation your friend got caught in." Raking a hand through his thick hair, he pushed back the mop hanging in front of his eyes. "We met. We had fun. We had sex. We had a great time. She died of natural causes. End of story."

"Is it?" *Is death really the end?*

"All right, let me put it another way." Unbelievable how he tried to give rational explanations to what defied any logic. "Your friend had a wonderful evening, loads of fantastic sex, then died."

He summed it up so neatly she almost felt stupid for even wondering.

"I agree that it was an untimely demise," he kept going smoothly. "But if it had to happen, wouldn't it be a great way to go? Wouldn't you choose it for yourself if you could?"

That did it!

There was an underlying challenge in his question she didn't appreciate at all. Who did he think he was?

"I'd have never chosen to die young." She scoffed, irritated at the awareness hitting her. "The problem isn't if she had a nice death. The problem is that she collided with someone who has a fucked-up karma!"

"Bad karma didn't kill your friend." He was plainly incensed. "Rotten luck did."

"I don't buy it." She held the point stubbornly, hoping he'd crumble and make a clean slate of it. "Eunice deserved more than what she got."

"Don't we all?" Breathing deeply, he regained a measure of control over himself. "But she wouldn't have gotten it from a one-night stand, which is all I can offer women."

"Oh, I know you're not the settling kind." *Who could be in this lifestyle?* "Yet, I can't believe you view women only as slaves or one-night stands."

"Has anyone ever told you you're a very persistent lady?" He eyeballed her defiantly.

"The Grand Master does all the time." She giggled.

"He must be a very patient man." Joining in the amusement, Adrien relaxed, and his guard dropped. "Very well, I'll let you in on a secret." He licked his lips as though in anticipation of what was to come. "All the women I've been with have been a let-down in the end."

"You mean in general or just on Halloween?" Kind of obvious, the man seemed bent on confusing her.

"Just on Halloween," he provided. "It's like I get the urge for something more than a mere slave. I want . . ." He shrugged. "I'm not sure what I want, but every Halloween, I go out and try to find it."

"Was that what you were doing with Eunice?" *Was this man unreal or what?* "You picked her up, hoping she'd turn out to be whatever it is your seeking."

"Yeah, something like that." He nodded carefully. "She wasn't, and when I left, I swear she was sleeping peacefully."

"It didn't occur to you that she might be dead?" Anxiously, she searched his face for signs that he was lying.

"No, why should it?" His expression looked too innocent

for words.

Reason why something warned her it might all be an act.

"Like everyone else I pick up at Halloween, she hadn't worked out," he carried on evenly. "That didn't mean she had to die or that I had something to do with it like you seem to be implying."

"I'm not . . ." The heat spreading on her face was probably painting it red. "I didn't —"

"Save it," he ordered curtly. "Do you think I hadn't seen where you're going with all your questions?"

"I just want to understand what happened to my friend," she repeated obstinately.

"Well, understand this," he snapped impatiently. "I'm not responsible for your friend's death." There was a new harsh edge in his tone. "I'm not looking for love." He spelled it out as though she were a child. "I'm most certainly not looking for soul mates."

"Then, why the Halloween craving?" Really hooked, she prodded, curious to get to the bottom of what appeared to be a certified puzzle.

"I don't know, and I don't care," he replied curtly. "For the sake of argument, even if I wanted to find a soul mate, how would I recognize her?"

Yvette raised the stakes. "What if it's a he?"

"A he?" A perplexed scowl marred his striking features. "What are you talking about?"

"That your soul mate isn't necessarily a woman." She elaborated. "It could just as well be a man." Then, raising her gaze, she regarded him intently. "Bet you never thought of that, did you?"

CHAPTER NINETEEN: ADRIEN

"**B**onjour, Adrien." Julia Le Clerque's dark head appeared from behind the stable door. "Is Pierre ready?"

"Yes, mademoiselle." Nearing the stall, Adrien Ascott tried to conceal his irritation.

It was Julia's third or fourth day back from that fancy school her parents had sent her to, and she'd been doing nothing except torment him.

"Here." Taking the reins, he led out a magnificent brown-coated gelding. "He's been fed, and he can't wait for some action."

He caressed the horse's neck affectionately. These beasts were about all he could stand of these awful Le Clerque, who thought themselves above mere mortals. With their money and influence, they could well afford it, which made him all the more furious with them.

"Thanks." Julia took the reins and led Pierre outside. "Would you give me a hand to mount?"

Too fat to do it yourself? Suppressing the snappy comeback, he hid his contempt. "Sure."

Up she went, with a little effort.

"Oh, Adrien." She turned lovesick, puppy brown eyes on him. "Would you mind accompanying me to the post office?"

He groaned.

In this day and age of 1890, when only ten years separated them from the turn of the twentieth century, women enjoyed the freedom they would've never imagined in France.

Why the hell was she bothering him?

"I'm sorry, mademoiselle." He worked hard to keep his voice even. "I've got work to do. Can't you ask your brother to go with you?"

"Marcel?" She said it like it was an alien come down from outer space rather than her brother. "Nah, he's busy." She pouted. "Besides, I much prefer your company."

Goddamn it. Adrien was just about fed up with her attitude. All he wanted from this odious family was revenge, or like the Marquis de Sade had so elegantly put it, "My vengeance needs blood." Le Clerque's blood, to be precise. Yet, he couldn't even plot in peace since she'd returned home and annoyed him with one silly errand after another.

To think he'd been working here for the past five years, ever since he'd been sixteen years old, and had hated every moment of it.

"My boy, we need more money," his father had told him the night that was to be his last one in the paternal home. "Monsieur Olivier Le Clerque saw you working in the fields and asked me if you'd be willing to see to his stables."

Behind the polite façade of his father's tone, Adrien knew that Olivier Le Clerque didn't ask. He ordered. What Olivier Le Clerque wanted, Olivier Le Clerque would get regardless of the obstacles standing in his way. In this case, regardless of all the loathing Adrien had felt for that degenerate family ever since he could remember. Maybe, the fact they had been successful and managed to come out of the French Revolution unscathed had something to do with it.

His family hadn't been so lucky. Annihilated from the senseless killings during the Reign of Terror, the last surviving member of what was once a wealthy and prominent family barely escaped with his head on his neck. Not a small feat everything considered, but alas, things had never been the same again. It was the reason André Ascott, Adrien's father, had been nothing better than a peasant, working the lands

Olivier Le Clerque owned outside of Aix-en-Provence.

The eleven mouths to feed hadn't helped, either. With nine brothers and sisters, Adrien's life had been excessive and crowded from the start, which had further depleted their meager resources. In other words, it explained why the Ascott family had nothing while Le Clerque had everything.

"Please, Adrien." Julia's pouting face came into sharp focus. "Why don't you come with me?"

"I told you, mademoiselle." Trying to be civil was proving to be a real challenge. "I'm busy."

For five years, Adrien had slaved under Le Clerque's thumb. That he'd wanted to rebel from the first day he'd started working in their abominable stables had been an understatement. That he hadn't, they owed to his father's unfortunate death, and his mother and unmarried sisters' sure demise had he not provided for them with his ridiculous wage.

Jean, his older and only surviving brother out of the original three, had inherited the land, but he had none of their father's experience. Plus, the doubling of the dues and taxes levied by Olivier Le Clerque had taken their toll. His mother and the three remaining sisters had also barely enough to eat. Safe to say, if the Ascott hadn't perished this time either, it had all been thanks to Adrien's hard-earned money as a stable hand.

No, make that as the stable keeper. After three years of service, three years of keeping his mouth shut, his head down, and working like a dog for someone who only deserved punishment for having all that he didn't, he'd been promoted.

"I don't believe you," Julia whined. "Adrien, why don't you like me?"

Slowly, he raised his gaze and realized the perfect means to get back at this worthless family was right there in front of him. For the first time ever, he understood what he read in Julia's bovine eyes. The fool was begging for a fraction of his attention, had been wanting it ever since she'd set foot back in the estate.

No, worse, the fool was in love with him. How long had that been going on?

He'd just noticed it, but neither knew nor cared. Then again, Julia Le Clerque had been a mere girl when he'd first arrived at the mansion, around ten or twelve, if he remembered correctly, which he didn't. Why should he?

The girl had been just one more pesky nuisance among the hundreds. He hadn't the slightest wish to get embroiled with her, not then. Not now, either, if he had to be honest, even if she wasn't a girl anymore.

Marcel had informed him that Julia had turned eighteen the day she'd returned to Aix-en-Provence and that she'd been betrothed to the Marquis René d'Amblairs.

On giving her a second inspection, Adrien had to agree that she appeared more mature than when he'd last checked. Grownup in every sense, including a thick waistline and robust frame that tantalized him with all those curves in all the right places. Big belly, plump breasts, and a round ass all his for the taking.

Not bad, he had to admit at his third glance, feeling the first stiffening of his penis at the thought that she was also a virgin, which was irrelevant for his purpose. She could've been a fat, ugly cow for all he cared. Good thing she was sweet, innocent, and plump enough for his cock to give her a standing ovation. Besides, she was to marry the Marquis René d'Amblairs.

What clinched it for him was that for some mysterious coincidence, she was so hung up on him that there was no hiding it. Could anything be more delicious or more useful?

CHAPTER TWENTY

" A drien." Julia Le Clerque dismounted. "Are you even listening to me?" Down on the ground, she approached
him tentatively.

"Why should I?" After tossing back his head, his long hair
fell behind his shoulders. "You're just another spoiled brat."
It didn't take much acting on his part to look angrier than he
felt. "Who thinks the world belongs to her only because she's
a Le Clerque!"

Spinning around, he went inside the stable, pretty sure
she'd run after him.

"No, wait." Too predictable, the silly woman rushed to follow. "Please, Adrien." Once inside, she grabbed his arm.
"Why don't you like me?"

"What makes you say that?" Changing register in the blink
of an eye. He was on her, pushing her against the nearest wall.
He pressed his weight to keep her trapped, something he
achieved without any sweat, for his six feet six easily towered
over her meager five feet.

"Maybe, I like you too much," he whispered seductively in
her ear.

"Really?" That her senses were reeling was evident from
the sudden flush coloring her cheeks and the brightness of her
dark eyes. "I thought I was just another brat —"

"You are." He licked the lobe of her ear. "That's why I need
to teach you a lesson."

"A lesson?" Her flesh quivering was a definite sign of excitement.

His own wasn't faring any better. What had begun like a half-mast cock was rapidly turning into a rigid beast full of demands.

"What kind of lesson?"

If she tried to be coy, she didn't quite succeed. Then again, Julia had no experience with men and not just because she was too young. She'd been imprisoned in a boarding school since forever.

"The hurting kind, of course." *'Cause that's the only lesson you deserve.*

Without giving her the chance to reply, he attacked her mouth like prey to be conquered. First, his tongue traced the edge of her rosy lips before opening them wide.

She didn't offer any resistance. Parting her warm cavity, she relinquished all control.

Plunging inside her mouth, he tasted her sweetness and became stone-like. His beefy monster dug a hole in her stomach, something he was sure she noticed even if no action seemed forthcoming. It didn't worry him in the least. He'd promised her discipline, and he would deliver one that would break her. Literally.

"Here." Pulling away, he clutched her hands and placed them around the thickness about to explode inside his breeches. "This will be your master from now on."

"My master?" She didn't have any idea of what was going on.

"Yes, you'll do whatever it demands." Slipping it out from its tight confinement, he went for the naked feel.

There was a gasp, soon followed by an awed, "Oh." After glancing downward, her mouth fell open. "It's huge."

It was. No questions about it. It was impressive, the girth as much as the length, and several women had already told him quite profusely.

"Caress it like this." Covering Julia's smaller hand, he slid them up and down rhythmically.

"It's so soft," she purred, getting the hang of it. "Yet, so hard." There was a faint trace of amazement that congealed him into marble solidity.

"You can't appreciate it with your hands alone." However delicious the movement, it was nothing more than the preliminary stage of his growing arousal. "You have to taste it."

"What?" Impossible though it was, her pupils became enormous black pools of shocked disbelief. "I don't understand."

"Nothing to understand." Brusquely pulling away, he pushed on her shoulders until she'd dropped to the floor. "Get on your knees now," he ordered.

She scrambled to obey.

"Good." He stroked her long dark hair before yanking it and throwing back her head. "Now, open your mouth and don't close it until I tell you to."

Her lips parted tentatively.

"Wider," he snapped.

She complied hurriedly.

Taking instant advantage, he thrust the tip of his erection between her lips.

More couldn't fit, unfortunately.

"I said, *open your goddamn mouth!*" Adrien snarled impatiently.

She coughed, but he was without pity. Without mercy, either, for he shoved regardless of her discomfort. The predictable result was that she gagged.

"Use your tongue," he instructed once he realized he wouldn't get very far without her cooperation. "And suck."

The difference was immediate. Adrien's cock slid more easily down her throat. Then her unskilled licks thickened it to an unbearable consistency. Soon, it would be unmanageable and require more depth. For sure, he couldn't linger for too long.

"No teeth," he barked when they grazed the fathead. "Ever!" Tugging her hair, he caught her gaze. "Do you understand?"

She nodded, and he admired the pretty picture she made with the colossal shaft stuck halfway inside her mouth.

"Now, suck harder." He let go of her head. "Use your hands, too."

It took a little coordination on her part, but she did a great job of it eventually.

Gustier laps had her lips pressing more firmly around his broad circumference. Her intakes became divine. Her palms sliding up and down nearly caused him to lose it. More than that, she was getting high on him.

He saw it every time she managed to gulp him down properly. The way her eyes shone was a sure sign she was enjoying it, which enabled his rod to reach her throat faster and easier. It was all too good, and it was about to overwhelm him, whether he wanted it or not. Clutching her head, he pinned it against the wall and pumped frantically.

Her gurgles were an extra turn-on that accelerated his tempo to the point of no return. Bending his knees, he drove his monster with double the impact power that first nailed her mouth, then had him explode.

Hell!

Who would've thought that fucking her face would prove to be so mind-blowing?

Chapter Twenty-One

"Goddamn it!" His legs about to buckle. Adrien had to steady himself before he could return his not-so-limp beast inside his pants and allow Julia to pull away.

Although she coughed and gagged on his juice, he was happy to report that much of it was already in her belly. As far as lessons went, this first one had gone very well, which didn't mean he was in any way through with her.

"Get up," he ordered curtly. "I want to see what you're like under those petticoats."

"I . . ." Another fit of coughing cut off her voice. "I . . . what if someone comes?" Getting a grip on herself, she raised enormous brown eyes to him.

He read panic, shock, excitement, and so many other conflicting emotions it was like looking at her naked soul. Something he cared not a fig about, which was why he hardened his voice, "No one will come at this hour." He snickered. "In case you haven't noticed, it's almost noontime, and your family has only one priority at the moment." Yeah, he knew all about Le Clerque's habits. "That's to eat."

At the news, Julia's expression changed. Gone the fear of discovery, she was plainly hungry for more sex.

"Come here," he snapped. "Turn around."

When she did, he saw the long line of buttons running from her neck to her waist.

Good God!

Her bulky riding outfit would be a nightmare to remove! Merely thinking of the effort it would entail wore him down without considering the difficulties of putting it back on once he was done. It was then that he decided the best strategy would be simply to raise the heavy mass of fabric and the hell with the complicated feminine fashion that required women to be inaccessible to any man, including their husbands.

"Lean on the hay." Several bales lay at her feet, so he left her to it while reaching for a leather crop hanging on a far wall. When he returned to her side, the sight of her ample behind tightened his cock again. Pushed up and out, it was magnificent, no question about it. Large and probably buttery, he knew he wouldn't rest until he possessed it.

Julia would resist for sure. All the women he'd been with had resisted but to no avail. It was his particular taste, and he'd never allowed their silly prejudices to stand in the way of his demands.

Like the Marquis de Sade had so aptly stated, "It is always by way of pain one arrives at pleasure." Adrien, for one, had always believed the Marquis knew all there was to know about domination and submission. It was the reason he admired him so much, had read everything he'd ever written, and strived to live by his standards.

"Now, let me see what you're hiding under all this useless cloth." Clutching the hem of her skirt, he tossed it up along with the infinite layers of petticoats.

Underneath, he glimpsed the long hose and stockings that were her last protective barriers.

"I hope you don't mind, dear, if I dispense with the rest of your attire in a way you might not approve of." Setting aside the crop, he took the knife he always kept at his waist and cut a square from the end of her corset downward.

"No, wait!" Julia almost screamed, trembling violently. "Please, Adrien." She sniffled. "Why are you doing this?"

"Isn't it obvious?" Undeterred, he continued to slice through the silky undergarments, being careful not to graze her skin.

"No." She sobbed, trying to move away.

"Hold still, dear." However mellifluous his tone, it had a steely edge that blocked Julia's attempts at freedom. "I wouldn't want to hurt you."

"Please, Adrien." Her sobs were about to turn hysterical. "Why are you doing this to me?"

"Because I love you." The lie slipped so easily he almost believed it himself.

His words had the desired effect.

"Really?" Julia immediately relaxed and went all limp and docile. "I didn't think you could stand me."

"It was an act." He strengthened the deception, hooking her line and sinker. "How do you think your family would take it if they knew I had such feelings for their precious daughter?"

"Papa would be really mad." She shivered as though she imagined Olivier Le Clerque's reactions. "And Marcel . . ." She was probably picturing her brother's fierce opposition. "Oh, he'd be mad —"

"He'd be furious," Adrien cut her off while focusing on the delicate task of gaining entry to her ass and cunt. "You see, my dear, I had no choice but to make it look like I couldn't stand you."

"Yes, I see."

The awe and trust in her tone almost made him feel ashamed of himself. Almost, yet not quite. The opportunity to deceive this naïve virgin was simply too alluring for him to ignore.

"Now, be still while I finish my work." Having obtained her submission, Adrien hurried to remove the annoying cloth.

The upper edges had already peeled off, so all he needed was to rip what clung to her thighs, and Julia's splendid derriere was revealed in all its magnificence. Exceedingly round and white, it gleamed in the pale light of the stable. Underneath, Julia's bush seemed in stark contrast, though his attention was drawn to the curve of her belly protruding above the dark pubic hair.

Irresistible!

She was sheer irresistible!

Tucking away his knife, he clutched those spectacular buns and squeezed hard to get the full feeling of them.

No surprise there.

They were soft and buttery like he'd envisioned. Uh, they were a delight that he would soon crack to satisfaction.

"Adrien, you're hurting me." Her high pitch snapped him out of the trance.

"Am I?"

Taking several breaths, he got a grip on himself. It would be foolish to waste this fabulous moment with a hurried possession, no matter how engrossed his piece had become at the idea of impaling the woman. He eased his hold.

"Sorry." Bending, he retrieved the leather crop. "It's just that you're beautiful." It was the only bit of truth he'd uttered since she'd appeared at the stable's door. "I fear I won't be able to control myself."

"What do you want to do to me?" The sheer excitement dripping from her husky voice wasn't hard to miss.

"Oh, too many things to list." He chuckled, taking a step back. "The first thing is to discipline you."

"Why?" The body that had been so relaxed a moment before went rigid all at once. "What have I done wrong?"

"Hush, dear." Aiming, he landed the first blow on her right buttock.

"Ouch!" Julia yelled and tried to raise her back.

"Don't move," he hissed, striking her other buttock. "And shut up." Since she didn't reply, he rewarded her with a kind caress of the same crop he'd used to inflict pain. "Now, listen." His tone went gentle once more. "This will hurt me more than it will you." Raising the crop, he brought it down hard like he would strike her again. At the last second, he stroked her flesh lovingly. "Believe me." To stress his point, he hit her fiercely.

Whack, whack, whack, whack.

The rapid succession left him breathless. Julia, too. Or maybe, she was in shock.

"The reason I'm doing this is that you are too much of a temptation." Observing the red splotches spreading on her lovely whiteness, he nearly came undone in his breeches. "I've had to repress my urges for far too long."

Commanding his cock to stand down wasn't all that easy. Still, he managed it.

"Which is unnatural for a man," he added more harshly. "Do you understand now why I have to punish you?"

Julia hesitated for a fraction of a moment. "I'm not—"

A terrible blow made her howl in pain.

"I didn't give you permission to speak." For good measure, he connected the crop a few more times to her delicious behind. "Do you understand?"

She didn't fall into his trap again and kept silent.

Having waited for her to slip up unsuccessfully, he granted at last, "You have permission to speak."

"Yes," she mumbled.

"Yes, *Master*." He slapped her lightly on the underside of her buttock. "That's how you'll address me from now on."

"Yes, Master," she repeated obediently.

"Now, let me return to my first question." Satisfied, he touched the red spots tenderly, relishing the feel of the heat warming his palm. "You are to blame for my state." Taking his shaft from its confinement, he rubbed it on her sore ass. "Feel this?"

Julia nodded.

Adrien bent to catch sight of her face. "Do you know what

it is?"

Kind of predictable, her face became purple.

"Well, do you?" Enjoying her discomfort, he pressed the whole of his engorged length on her backside. "I give you permission to say it."

"Your penis," she squeaked feebly.

"It's called *cock*." He struck her since she'd got it wrong. "It's all your fault if it's so hard." Another couple of thwacks were in order. "Tell me, do you understand your punishment?"

"Yes, Master." She sounded disconsolate.

"You're also enjoying this way too much." He deliberately raised the stakes, already anticipating her fierce denial. "Which is another reason I'm doing this."

"Not true!" Julia exploded, unable to contain herself.

"Liar!" He knew it better than her since he had no trouble spotting the glistening in her pussy. "You're nothing but a liar!" After hitting her twice for talking without his express consent, he stuck a couple of fingers in her cunt and withdrew them thoroughly drenched. "This is how wet you are." He slid them slowly on her skin so that she would have no doubts.

There was no describing her embarrassed silence. Adrien could practically feel the shame befuddling her already confused mind.

"Are you or are you not a slut?" Adrien insisted cruelly. "It's obvious you are," he taunted as he brushed her throbbing clit and puffed-up labia. "It's clear you're in bad need of chastisement." He snickered. "Wouldn't you agree?"

CHAPTER TWENTY-TWO

Defeated, Julia slumped on the bale of hay she was using for support.

"Ah, ah, ah." Adrien's vicious spank had her bolting upright again. "I didn't allow you to lower your back."

She wailed in frustration. "But—"

"Hush." The leather crop crackled as it whipped the air before landing squarely on her ass. "Shut your mouth and listen." Going to stand in front of her, he bent and cupped her face between his palms. "You shouldn't feel ashamed for liking what I'm doing or being so wet for it. It's a natural reaction." Softly, he removed a mop of brown hair from her eyes and noticed from their shine how close to tears she was. "Have you ever heard of the Marquis de Sade?"

Her eyes grew huge.

"So, you've heard of him," he mused. "Did the girls in that fancy school of yours talk about him?"

She nodded slowly, her gaze never wavering from him.

"What exactly did they say?" Curiosity had the better of him.

Julia didn't rush to satisfy him.

"I gave you an order, slut." His voice turned harsh as he regarded her coldly. "When your master orders, you obey." He yanked her hair in the most hurtful way possible. "Got it?"

"Yes, yes," she croaked.

"Yes, what?" He eased the pressure.

"Yes, Master," she replied dutifully.

"Good." Letting her hair go, he caressed her face. "Now,

what did your school friends think of the Marquis de Sade?"

"That he's a monster," Julia whispered uneasily. "That he causes pain on purpose because he must be sick or something."

"How wrong they are, my dear." Chuckling, he straightened. "The Marquis de Sade is the sole man I admire." Retracing his steps, he returned to stand behind her exposed ass and cunt. "Because he alone knows women for what they truly are."

"What would that be?" Given her steady tone, she'd been evidently encouraged by his previous gentleness.

"Sluts." Deciding to withhold punishment for speaking out of turn, he massaged the giant ass cheeks. "They're all sluts whose only purpose is to be slaves and serve their masters in every way possible."

"Why the pain?" As though possessing a mind of its own, her butt inched up and back to deepen his stroking.

"The Marquis said, *The only way to a woman's heart is along the path of torment,* and he's right." He stimulated the clit swimming in a thick honeydew of desire, relishing her thighs tightening around his fingers. "I gave you a trashing you'll never forget, yet here you are." The pink swell was about to burst from sheer pleasure. "Begging for more."

"This is wrong!" Julia cried in dismay. "I can't be so bad that—"

"The Marquis also said, *To know virtue, we must first acquaint ourselves with vice.*" Adrien licked his lips. "That's what I'm teaching you." Traveling from her clit to her pussy, his fingers sank into her silky trap. "To recognize your vices." Then, he went further upward and hovered on her ass ring. "Because if you don't, how will you ever know what true virtue is?" His middle finger plunged in the exceedingly cramped confinement of her virgin ass.

She moaned in response as he increased the pressure to

three digits.

"Yes, this will do nicely," he confirmed, twisting to enlarge the narrow hole. "After I've taken care of this other very interesting cavity of yours." Leaving the snug confinement of her derriere, he slipped several fingers in her swamped slit.

"I can't." All fearful, she tensed her muscles. "I have to marry the Marquis René d'Amblairs."

"Do you love him?"

Of course, he didn't give a crap if she did. He was counting on this engagement to wreck Le Clerque's reputations once and for all.

"Hem . . ." Her hesitation confirmed his ploy was working. "Not really," she admitted at last.

"So, why worry?" Triumphant, he began a rhythmical screwing of her pussy. "Didn't you always want to do this with someone you loved?"

He could easily imagine her silly fantasies and the daydreams she must've shared with those fools of her school friends.

"I did," she confessed. Then, she twisted to catch Adrien's gaze. "You do love me, Adrien, don't you?"

He was severely tempted to crush the emotional undercurrent he read in her eyes, but it would mean the end of his control.

"Of course, I do." He lied instead. "Now, if you stop looking at me, I'll show you how much."

Compliant, Julia returned her gaze to the wall in front of her.

Great!

His cock as rigid as a rock, Adrien rubbed the fathead on her puffed-up folds to get it wet enough.

She responded enthusiastically, throwing back her ass and increasing their closeness until he pushed to enter.

Two things happened at once. Adrien felt her barrier and

shoved to get past it. She stopped moving for the time it took him to rip her virginity apart. Then, she screamed and attempted to escape.

"Hush." Reaching forward, he clamped a hand over her mouth. "And breathe." Stuck inside her, he couldn't help enjoying how narrow she felt and wished he could push some more. "I don't want to hurt you, but there's no easy way to do this." Sliding to his balls, the whole of his beast became embedded in her. "If you promise to keep your mouth shut, I'll make you like it a whole lot more."

She nodded, and he removed his hand.

Slipping it beneath her soft belly, he traced its sexy curve before zeroing on the tight bud above her pussy lips. One brush and the woman lost it. Rocking herself, she thrust back, impaling his beefy monster to the root while begging for more.

Itching from the need to fuck her good and proper, he grabbed one of her arms. "You can do this yourself," he commanded, bringing her hand between her legs and letting it go. "While I finish up here."

"I . . ." Unconvinced, she hesitated, raising her hand so that it remained in midair. "I can't." Helplessly, her arm fell back down.

"Suit yourself." Uncaring of whatever ridiculous dilemma she was grappling with, Adrien gripped her hips and shoved with all the impact power he could muster. "It's your problem, so don't come crying to me if I hurt you."

Her response was to tense all over and tightened her legs, something that evidently brought her a measure of fulfillment judging from the way she eased his penetration.

As he slammed for greater depth, his giant girth inevitably occupied all the space she had available. She was nice and tight.

Nice and exploding, actually, from the effort of

accommodating a piece way too big for her limited cunt, which had adapted surprisingly fast and gave him full access.

Most astonishing, though, was seeing how much she relished his fucking. It made all the difference, especially when the frantic convulsing of everything told him she'd reached the maximum pleasure.

Uh, it was too much!

Delicious and mind-blowing all at once, he pumped a few more times, then shot his load to her belly.

CHAPTER TWENTY-THREE

"Don't you dare move," Adrien snarled, still stuck in her as stiff as before his unbelievable orgasm.

Julia looked too limp to budge. Still, he was in no way finished with her.

"Now, we have the last part of your initiation." Retrieving his stick from her soaked pussy wasn't as easy as he'd thought. So snug and comfy, he wished he could leave it there forever. Thank God, he would soon conquer an even more enticing position than the one he was abandoning.

"Do you hear me?" For good measure, he slapped her generous buttocks that were still bright red from the earlier beating.

"Yes, Master," she acknowledged wearily.

"This time, you won't scream," he warned threateningly. "Right?"

"No, Master," she confirmed meekly. "I'm sorry I did it before."

"Not to worry." With what was to come, he could afford to be magnanimous. "You'll receive the punishment you deserve." His erection jerked in blatant anticipation of what he was about to do.

"Please, Master, don't hurt me anymore." As though guessing where this was going, she trembled.

"Hurt you?" Pushing down on her backside, he spread her buns and slid his cock in between the crack. "I only want to take what's mine."

Rubbing his massive fathead naturally increased his desire

to impale her guts ruthlessly, without any preambles. Not that he would get away with it. Julia was proving to be a fragile creature who needed constant reassurances. To do his bidding, he had to convince her it would be the best thing for her.

"This is also the ultimate test." This new twist would speed up matters, which wouldn't be such a bad deal considering how late the hour must've grown, not to mention how frightfully higher the risk of discovery before he'd taken all she had to give.

"To verify that you really love me as much as you say you do." A couple of fingers slipped through her narrow ring and rotated to enlarge it.

"I do, Adrien." She was almost sobbing. "I swear it."

"I don't need swearing." Unmoved, he continued to ravage her behind with a third digit added to the mix. "I need proof." He loved how tight she was. "That's why I order you to touch yourself." This time, he wouldn't take no for an answer, however much he pretended it was the grandest concession of his life.

"W . . . what?" Like before, she stuttered helplessly. "Touch myself?" She sounded as horrified as if he'd suggested she kill herself. "What do you mean?"

Right, how to forget this cow had probably never done what came natural to more experienced women?

"It means that you place your hand here." Wrenching her arm roughly, he directed it in between her legs.

"No, it isn't right." Quickly retrieving it, she flattened it against her breast.

"Nonsense!" Of course, he wouldn't stand for any disobedience, especially since it would've been the second on the same day. "Put that fucking hand back where I told you." At her hesitation, he almost yelled, "Do it *now!*"

"I . . . I . . ." Her hand fluctuating between her belly and legs would've been comical, had he cared for any humor.

"They told me it isn't proper. That God disapproves and will punish me."

"I'll punish you, slut, if you don't comply right now," he stated flatly.

She flinched as though he'd slapped her.

"Get your goddamn hand between your legs." He scoffed impatiently. "Or I swear I—"

"Here." Her hand landed right smack on the dark pelvis hair. "Please, don't get mad."

"I won't as long as you do exactly as I say."

It was difficult to describe how arousing the sight was. Safe to say, Adrien's shaft twitched visibly in evident enjoyment.

"Do it. Stroke yourself." He concluded harshly.

"Where?" It was hard to tell whether she was playing dumb or simply had no idea of what she was supposed to do.

"Lower, dear." God! How he was tempted to explode and give her a piece of his mind. "Dig under the hair and bury your fingers in your wetness." Instead, he managed to keep a cool façade.

Her digits slid unhurriedly toward the center of her pleasure and became entangled in the thick curly hair. "Is this all right?"

There was a note of defiance he was sure he'd eliminate given enough time, agony, and training.

"Listen, slut," he snapped. "Don't play coy with me," he cautioned menacingly. "I'm doing you a favor and allowing you to experience more than the pain I'll now inflict upon you." For good measure, he rammed four fingers in her narrow butt opening, so fiercely, she jumped.

"Suit yourself," he jeered in irritation.

Enough of her. It was time to satisfy his primal urges, and Adrien had a soft, buttery, quite conspicuous derriere to help him forget all the hatred he felt for Le Clerque's family.

Removing his fingers, he targeted the puckered entrance

with a crown grown too big for words.

Yeah, all this excitement was getting to him. Tightening his grip on the buttocks he was keeping firmly apart, he thrust and slipped.

"Damn!" He was too saturated. That was the problem. His problem, to be precise, though it soon became hers. "Don't move." He huffed as if it were her fault. "I need you to keep still."

That Julia hadn't budged was irrelevant.

Taking a second aim, he shoved and nailed the hole good and proper. From Julia's muffled cry, he guessed she wasn't too pleased by it, but he was beyond caring about her. It was simply too good to fling this spectacular ring wide open, cracking it under the pressure of a giant beast screwing its entire fabulous length into it.

There was no way of describing the sheer bliss enveloping him on every side. Amazing and incredible at the same time, he pumped more fiercely, and the ass rewarded him. Bit by bit, it yielded to his vigorous pounding until he was balls deep into the tastiest cramped confinement he'd ever known.

Julia's mood had also switched. From resistance, she'd gone to liking his steady hammering and testified it by decisive throwbacks of her own.

Too fabulous to last for much longer, he felt the juice rise. A couple of more shoves and he was history. The load pressing at the tip of his erection burst in an unstoppable stream of liquid ecstasy that had him collapse on her behind and hold on for dear life.

Then, depleted and utterly fulfilled, he let her go and sank to the ground.

CHAPTER TWENTY-FOUR

"Adrien, do you know where my sister is?" Marcel Le Clerque's large face suddenly came into sharp focus. Charging into the stables, he looked around as though she were hiding there.

To say that he was big was an understatement. He'd always resembled a pig more than a man. About the same age as Adrien, his fat belly protruding over thick short legs and round, pudgy face marked him as belonging to the hogs' species rather than that of the humans.

"We've been looking for her all over."

"Sorry, sir." All deferential and submissive, Adrien didn't even bother to look him in the eyes. "She isn't here."

"What about her horse, Pierre?" Swinging his gaze frantically, Marcel landed it on a distant stall. "Is he here?"

"All horses are here and accounted for." Adrien had made sure of it.

Good thing he'd insisted on bringing back Pierre after he'd persuaded the deluded fool that was Julia into abandoning everything and everyone. It avoided unwanted questions and unauthorized reappearances.

"She hasn't been here to take Pierre." He stared in the direction of the magnificent brown-coated gelding. "I haven't seen her for the past couple of days."

"Do you know where she might be?" Marcel insisted, suspicion clouding his gaze.

"No, sir," Adrien lied smoothly. "Why should I know?"

Of course, he knew where Julia was. At the Belle Fleure

Inn, located in Sainte-Marie-Lilac, a village just five miles from Aix-en-Provence. First, he'd convinced her to elope with him before her wedding day. Then, he had arranged her stay at the Belle Fleure, promising he'd join her after a few days of settling things at the estate.

In other words, he'd organized their escape to the last detail. Too bad, the silly cow had no idea he didn't intend to keep his side of the bargain, not even after her disappearance was two days old.

That had been the plan, after all.

His plan, not hers, naturally. The woman would wait in vain. The wedding wouldn't take place. The Le Clerque family would be ruined. Adrien's triumph would be complete.

"'Cause she's always hanging around the stable," Marcel huffed, annoyed.

"I assure you, sir." Adrien raised his gaze. "She seldom speaks to me."

Except for when she begged him not to hurt her.

Months had passed since he'd first tasted her sweetness, months in which he'd trained her body to the finer points of pain and pleasure.

Against his better judgment and his initial resolve, he had liked it far more than he would've ever imagined.

No, he liked *her*, the damnable Julia Le Clerque with all her sinewy curves, her insufferable insecurities, her intoxicating compliance.

In a sense, he'd mastered her, turned her into a perfect slave.

Yet, in another sense, she'd enslaved him to her addictive ingenuity. It hadn't stopped him from proceeding with his revenge.

"Is that a fact?" Marcel eyed him with more distrust than before. "There has been some talk — "

"Malicious gossip, sir," Adrien rushed to deny. "Nothing

true there, believe me."

"Fact is no one has seen her since the day before yesterday." Dropping his skeptical attitude, the prized heir of the odious family now looked like a lost little boy. "Today is All Hallows Eve, and the Marquis René d'Amblairs, her fiancée, has arrived. Tomorrow, on All Saints, she's supposed to marry him." He wrung his hands in agitation. "Guests are also pouring in from everywhere, but there's no trace of the bride." Pacing around the stable, he came to a stop in front of him. "Do you understand why we must find her?"

"I totally understand," Adrien forced his voice to be even, working hard to keep his glee at bay. "But I can't help you."

"Goddamn it!" Marcel punched the stable door in a fit of rage. "Goddamn women and whoever invented them!"

"Wasn't it the Good Lord?" Adrien sought to provoke him on purpose.

"I'm beginning to think it was Satan himself," Julia's brother retorted angrily.

"Then, maybe, he could tell you where your sister is," Adrien offered slyly.

"I wish he could." After another look over the empty place save for Adrien and the horses, Marcel whirled around. "Do come and tell me if she turns up," he ordered as he stormed out, headed toward the main house.

When hell freezes over, you swine! "Sure will," he replied instead to the man's massive back. "And good riddance," he added low enough that no one would hear.

CHAPTER TWENTY-FIVE

"Was that the master?" A chubby brunette came out from the side room where he lived, half-naked from her waist down.

"Nah, it was just Marcel." Spinning around, Adrien admired her plump form, as round and curvy as he liked it.

"He's a master, too," she chided gently. "Maybe, I should go back to the house to see if they need—"

"Not a chance, Nadine." Taking the maid's arm, he dragged her back to the room. "We've got unfinished business."

"I might help." The woman resisted his pull. "If they can't find Mademoiselle Julia—"

"Your presence won't make a bit of a difference." Applying more force got Nadine through the door. "Besides, too many people are already looking for her. You'd only add to the confusion." With another decisive push, he threw her on the bed.

Falling on her belly, she conceded. "Maybe, you're right."

"I'm always right."

The sight of her round ass was magnificent. Well, maybe not as much as Julia's, but Adrien suppressed all thoughts of her.

"That's why I'm the master." To dispel any more unwanted paragons, he spanked the generous derriere a couple of times.

"You certainly are," Nadine purred mischievously.

"Glad you agree." Unfastening the buttons of her corset, he removed it before slapping the firm buttocks twice more.

"Now, turn around, so I can show you how masterful I can be."

She immediately tensed. "Will you hurt me."

"Oh, honey." Squeezing the considerable mass he couldn't wait to possess, he leaned over to whisper seductively in her ear, "You know I will."

It was the only way he liked his women, pliant and submissive, ready for pain or pleasure, depending on his fancy.

"Come on." Straightening, he made sure he wasn't touching her anymore. "I haven't got all day."

"Yes, Master." Sighing, she finally flipped on her back, and he had a clear view of her medium-sized breasts, dark bush, and shapely legs. All in all, she wasn't bad, though she wasn't Julia and had none of the allure of Le Clerque's offspring if he had to be honest.

Good thing, his cock didn't seem to care. It had stiffened the moment it had caught sight of Nadine's naked ass and was as rigid as a stone.

"Open your legs."

When she obeyed, her clit swam in an ocean of honeydew. Great news.

She was still wet from his earlier fondling despite Marcel's accursed interruption.

Yeah, the man had the worst timing possible. He'd stormed in as Adrien had been about to plunge his stick into her. Naturally, he'd pick up where he'd left off before.

Kneeling in front of Nadine, Adrien raised her legs to his shoulders. The puckered entrance beckoned, and there was no stopping him. With one well-aimed thrust, he flung it open. Then, heedless of her grimaces of pain, he continued screwing until the whole long length of him was safely embedded in her cramped and fiery sheath, balls slapping the outside of her buttocks.

Heaven!

It had to be what heaven felt like if it existed.

"Master," her voice was a squeak. "Can I touch myself?"

No question about it. Nadine was as well-trained as you could get. She'd learned that she had to ask permission for everything. Also to talk, come to think of it.

"Who gave you permission to speak?" Playing it cruel, he slammed deeper into her.

She went all red in the face but kept her mouth shut.

"Just for that." In and out, he was enlarging the once tiny opening to the satisfaction of his considerable girth. "I forbid you from taking any initiatives."

Her dark eyes begged him openly, and he wondered whether to be merciful for once. It was true that women craved pain like the Marquis de Sade loved to remind, but sometimes a little mercy could go a long way in the road of a man's pleasure.

He dipped two fingers in the pool that was her pussy and rubbed the throbbing swell hidden beneath the dark hair. "Would this be what you want to do?"

Nadine gasped from the shock of his unexpected gesture.

"Tell me." He stroked her more forcefully before sticking three fingers in her soaked slit.

"Yes, Master," she muttered out of breath.

"Have you earned it by any chance?" Switching back to the role of a ruthless Dom, he removed his wet fingers and impaled her with his erection to her guts, pumping steadily to go beyond the obvious confinements.

"No, Master." That this awareness crushed her was undeniable.

"Then, why should I let you?" Noticing how taut her nipples had become, he reached over and twisted them brutally.

She nearly jumped, only he was too deep inside for her to go anywhere except around his twitching monster.

"Because I promise I'll be good," she squealed. "No, better

from now on."

"Why should I believe you?" Adrien teased, getting a kick out of squeezing her tight rosy buds.

"Because . . ." She tried to come up with a good excuse and utterly failed.

For the fun of it, he zeroed in on her cunt once more. He was so close to a tremendous come that he might as well do everything himself this time.

"All right, slut." He brushed her velvety pussy with frantic slides. "Come for me." He rammed her behind. So fiercely, the slap of his crotch on her buttocks resounded like a loud clap.

This double deal accelerated things and spun them out of any control. Nadine was the first to crack under pressure. Digging her head on the straw mattress, she howled her orgasm to the world.

He wasn't far behind. Splitting Nadine's ass always did that to him. Pounding her a couple of more times was the end of him. The juice rose, and he pulled out in time to unload on her white skin, smearing her stomach and breasts with whitish spunk.

To make sure not a drop remained, he jerked his shaft until he caught the flicker of a movement with the corner of an eye. He turned.

Julia!

Mute and pale, the would-be bride stood for a second on the threshold with huge eyes full of pain and hurt. Before he had the chance to do anything, she whirled around and was gone.

CHAPTER TWENTY-SIX

"Julia!" Bolting upward and throwing on the first pair of pants that came his way, Adrien rushed out of the room. "Wait!"

Goddamn her!

What was she doing here? How dare she come back and spoil his carefully planned revenge?

The stable door banged shut, so he followed her outside.

The woman wasn't far away, running up a hill on the left side. With his long legs and more powerful muscles, it was no hardship for him to catch her.

"Wait," he repeated, detaining her. "What the fuck are you doing here?"

"Me?" That she was furious was evident from her extreme pallor and the trembling of her lips. "What are you doing with Nadine?"

"I was doing what I do best." He scoffed haughtily. "Being a master."

"With her?" Julia raised her voice. "I thought I was your only slave."

"You thought wrong." Playing it cruel and insensitive was sure to hurt her even more than she already was.

"I don't understand." Deflated, she lowered her voice to a whisper, "Didn't you say you loved me?"

"Did I?" He shrugged indifferently. "I don't recall."

"Are you saying you don't love me, Adrien?" Slowly, she searched his face for any sign of that elusive love she was so fond of and that he never believed in, no matter what he said.

"Masters don't love their slaves," he sneered. "I thought you had gotten that by now."

"I . . . I . . ." Dumbfounded, she batted her eyelids. "I love you."

"That's your problem." He spat, unsympathetic about her fate.

"I did everything you told me," she insisted as though it could be grounds for being loved.

"You're a slave," he reminded. "You have no other choice except to obey me."

"But . . . but . . ."

There she went again, looking at him like a deer about to be slaughtered.

"I broke my vows to the Marquis René d'Amblairs."

"Again, my dear, it's your problem." Realizing she was too defeated to go anywhere, he let her go.

"We were to elope." Her voice was growing hysterical. "I waited for you at Belle Fleure."

"I have no wish to elope with you." He spelled out the words, so there'd be no margins for misunderstanding. "Never had." He snickered. "Why should I waste my life with the likes of you?" He looked her up and down as if she were dirt. "You're no good as a slut. You're not even good enough to be a slave." Every detail he was piling on her was like another nail in her coffin. "Hell, Nadine is better at both than you'll ever be, and she's no lady, just a cleaning woman."

"But . . ." Her mouth opened and closed without emitting the slightest sound.

Which brought to mind a fish thrown out of the water, thrashing to catch its last breath.

"But . . ." Julia gave it another try, seemingly out of breath and of things to say. "I . . . I'm pregnant!"

Well, this was news to him.

"Congratulations. Who is the father?" Adrien challenged,

knowing well it could be only him.

"Adrien!" Shocked, she stared at him as though he were a ghost or something. "You know it's yours."

"Is it?" Coolly, he spun around to return to the stables. "I hate to repeat myself, but again, it's your problem."

"No, wait." Scurrying after him, she clutched his arm. "You don't understand." She tightened her grip, probably fearing he'd go without listening. "You see, I don't just love you and carry your child." Her eyes widened under the strain of many conflicting emotions. *"You are my soul mate."* She emphasized it as though it would explain everything.

"Your soul mate?" He laughed out loud. *Could anything be more ludicrous?* "That's the most ridiculous thing I've heard in all my life." To stress how foolish she was, he locked his gaze on hers. "There is no such thing as a soul mate. It doesn't exist."

"It does," she spat out heatedly. "I know 'cause you're mine."

"Prove it," he mocked.

"Didn't you feel it when we met the first time?" She glanced at him, all adoring. "Didn't you feel a spark of recognition? Didn't you feel like we had met before?"

"I felt a spark of hate," he confessed brutally. "Does that qualify?"

"I don't understand." Her feeble attempt to pretend she hadn't heard what he said didn't move him. Not one bit.

"What's there to understand?" He got ready to shred her last illusions to bits. "I hate you, Julia, and I despise your family." There, he'd admitted it loud and clear. "Do you understand now?"

Crestfallen, the air blew out of her sails, and the hand clasped on his arm dropped to her side.

He took immediate advantage of her lost expression to get the hell out of there.

"No." Suddenly finding herself, she grabbed his arm once more. "You can't walk away now, not after everything I told you."

Spinning around, he confronted her. "What do you want me to do? I have nothing to offer you, no money, and no job if your family finds out."

"You said you didn't care about the money." She was quick to retrieve some of the things he'd used to convince her to elope. "You said that our love would be enough. That you'd find a job somewhere else, and that we'd live happily ever after."

"I've said a good many things I didn't believe," he snapped before removing her paw from his arm and striding away. "As things stand, I'll deny having anything to do with you."

"You are my soul mate," she repeated mechanically. "There's something between us that goes beyond this life."

"That's all a pile of crap they taught you at that fancy and useless school of yours." Adrien huffed. "The only things between us were your cunt and ass." He offended her deliberately.

"No, it can't be." She reeled back from the blow, and he took his chance to leave her. "No, Adrien, you can't go." Again, she tried to detain him, but he didn't allow it, his unbroken stride swiftly increasing the distance between them. "What am I to do?" Julia croaked, and he imagined her horror-stricken face from the consequences of what would soon be manifested.

"You could always crawl back to your Marquis and beg him to take you back." He snorted contemptuously. "Maybe, he'll also raise your bastard son."

"You are a monster!" She staggered back as though this last remark had undone her utterly and totally. "You are a fiend!" she shrieked. "Worse than anything that's going to roam the Earth tonight!"

Right, tonight was All Hallows Eve?

Her voice increased a notch, "I hate you, Adrien Ascott!"

At the realization that she'd been betrayed, something had broken loose in her, and she couldn't hold anything back anymore. The flood of her rage gushed out like an unstoppable torrent from a dam that had ruptured.

"Do you hear me?"

If she kept yelling, it was because he hadn't even bothered slowing down at her great turn-about. He kept marching away.

"I hate you!" Julia repeated with more conviction. "You just used me! You never cared for me! You are the most insensitive lout I've ever had the misfortune of knowing!"

She could shout all she liked. Adrien didn't care. His revenge was perfect as it was, with the bonus of a pregnancy he hadn't expected. It made it all so much more delicious, especially if he pictured the Marquis and Le Clerque's embarrassment when they'd realize they'd been duped.

"For the final time, my dear, it's your problem." Without turning back, he kept striding toward the stables, glad to be rid of her once and for all.

CHAPTER TWENTY-SEVEN

The ending of Julia Le Clerque's sad tale was predictable to a fault.

She hung herself. What else could she have done?

Her life was ruined, and so was Le Clerque's name. Everything had worked out perfectly had it not been for that nagging sensation. What it was exactly, he had no idea.

He only knew that he missed her.

Yeah, wasn't that crazy?

He fucking missed her!

Fat, naïve, sweet, innocent Julia.

Incredible!

No, ironic if he had to be precise. Could it have something to do with that other trifle that had happened to him? That trifle that had made him immortal?

Yes, that was what he'd become — an immortal!

There could be no other explanation. He was alive in 2020 while born in 1869. In other words, if math wasn't an opinion, he was one hundred and fifty-one years old. Best of all, he hadn't aged a day from his twenty-first birthday.

Like Oscar Wilde's Dorian Gray, he maintained his beautiful appearance regardless of his vices, which could be a good thing. Or bad, depending on the point of view.

Maybe, his birthday being on All Hallows Eve, or Halloween as it was now called, had something to do with it?

For a long time, he'd thought it might have. Wasn't it a magical time, after all, a pillar of Celtic's pagan culture that had spilled into Catholic beliefs?

Oh, all right, the Christians had extended the period until the second day of November. By adding an All Saints and All Souls days, they thought they had covered all the bases.

It made no difference.

They were all spirits that had broken loose from whatever immaterial dimension kept them trapped for the rest of the year, which substantiated the similarities. What it all boiled down to was superstitious credence in dead souls walking among us as though still alive. Whether passed off as demons, saints, or plain, old, regular folks, this Halloween business was all about death and the insane notion that life could continue after it.

All crap as far as he was concerned, but could it explain why he hadn't died so far? Could it be that those born on Halloween acquired some kind of magical property?

At first, he'd held on to that interpretation, convinced it was some kind of prize from above. When he remained all alone, when the people he'd cared about like his mother, sisters, and nephews all died, he wasn't so sure it was such a reward. More of a curse as time went by for everyone except for him. Yes, everyone died except for him, and everyone grew older while he still looked and felt twenty-one.

Well, not always.

There were times in a year when his façade slipped, and he looked more fiftyish than twentyish. The closer it got to Halloween, the more he aged, visibly decaying as he approached the turning of another year. His birthday would come and go, he'd do what he had to do to survive, and he would be his young self again.

Since he felt no shame or remorse, he hadn't pursued the reason for his uniqueness until it had dawned on him that he was a demon, damned for all of eternity in an endless loop of putrefaction, death, and rejuvenation. Completely shackled, he had no choice except to repeat the same cycle over and over without ever being able to break free.

He hadn't been too thrilled about this notion. Yet, he couldn't stop, for there seemed to be no way around the terrible things he had to do to stay alive one more year.

Why else would he have to sacrifice a pretty young thing every Halloween?

CHAPTER TWENTY-EIGHT

The first time it had happened had been during All Hallows Eve after Julia's death.

Adrien had been feeling weary and weak. Out of energy was more like it, as though something had sucked it all out of him. His first impulse had been to sleep it off, but Nadine waiting for him in the stables, naked and ready to spend the night with him, had changed his plans. A special birthday present, she'd promised, and it did turn out to be quite extraordinary.

Not for poor Nadine, alas.

After a whole night's worth of fulfilling sex, he'd woken up refreshed and feeling more alive than ever. Nadine, instead . . . well, she was dead. How that had happened, he had no idea. He hadn't struck her, hadn't slit her throat, hadn't drunk her blood.

Nothing!

He'd done nothing out of the ordinary, nothing besides the extreme sex he loved.

Yet, there it was—her inanimate corpse cold in his bed. Since that fateful All Hallows Eve, the deaths had been like clockwork. Every Halloween, he'd get exhausted and old, with a face so drawn he hardly recognized it. All it took to return to his perfect good looks and well-being was a night of passion with a maiden of his choice. Once through with her, he'd be fine. She'd be dead.

Like his latest fatality—Eunice Saint Jacques.

The woman with a keen sense of humor and an

encyclopedic knowledge of history had been too enticing to resist. He'd allowed nature to run its course until he'd woken up and found her dead.

Just like all the others. Only this time, Adrien had felt the loss of such a beautiful and intelligent woman. That these women all met their end because of him hadn't quite registered. At first, he'd put it down to unlucky coincidences or bad health. Only after the pattern kept repeating, again and again, had he begun to wonder. Was it his fault?

Seeing how things turned out, it probably was. Question was, what was it about him that required the taking of life? Why did he have to deplete these women until they couldn't take another breath?

Kind of like a vampire, only he was after their energy, and the exchange took place during their fabulous sex. In other words, he'd become a monster stealing innocent women's life source, but why did it happen only during Halloween?

Damn if he knew!

Damn if he cared, either.

It was simply a matter of survival. Nothing he could do would stop this deadly loop, nothing short of killing himself, which wasn't an option.

He simply had to do it to stay alive. No other explanation was possible. Was he despicable?

Probably yes, but no more than your average vampire who, in the end, had a much deadlier appetite than Adrien ever would. Plus, his casualties had loads of fun before dying, which didn't excuse what he did to them but made him feel a little better about it.

Oh, all right, it wasn't much of a consolation. Still, it kept Adrien going, undetected and unpunished since his annual killings were never classified as murders. How could they have been?

The victims always looked so peaceful that no one ever

suspected foul play.

Thank God for that, and one less thing he had to worry about in his one hundred and thirty years of activity. On the downside, he was getting bored, losing his taste for it. The unending repetition grated on his nerves more than he would've dared admit to himself.

He was also tired of living as he was, alone, without purpose, going from one meaningless sacrifice to the other. The only thing that had given him a measure of satisfaction had been his improved skills as a master, though they meant little if he didn't have the right slave for it, a slave who was destined to die in the long run, so what was the point of training it?

Besides, what was the point of any meaningful relationship if he would always outlive the other? Could this account for the emptiness in his life? Mostly, why had it all come back after only five minutes of talking with Yvette Carlisle, the Grand Master's slave at Club Sortilege?

In front of her, he'd held on firmly to the conviction that all her conjectures were nothing except absurd. Now, he wasn't so sure.

What if the problem was with his choices? What if she was right, and he'd been targeting the wrong gender all along?

CHAPTER TWENTY-NINE

"Welcome back, Master Ascott." Tony Spencer, Grand Master of Club Sortilege, bowed to him. "I trust you had a pleasant Presentation Night."

"It was excellent." Adrien nodded, remembering the event of the past week. "I hope I've gained your confidence now."

"Absolutely!" Tony smiled. "I hope you understand I had to do it since you were a new member, and that's what our rules require. Masters Devon and Sylvien vouched for you. Now you can enjoy full privileges here at Club Sortilege."

"I quite understand." Adrien nodded. "Thank you." He looked past the entrance to the rest of the large hall. "Where are the new slaves of the month?"

What he meant to ask was, "Where's that cute redhead I pretended to discard?"

For he'd been among the three chosen, along with the curvy brunette Adrien had disciplined.

The young man had struck him from the start. Though men weren't usually his thing, this one seemed different, lingering in his mind far more than any other slave. Still, he wouldn't have given him a second thought had it not been for Yvette's question. He couldn't wait to set eyes on this particular slave and determine whether something was there besides his wishful fancy.

"In three separate chambers at the back." Turning around, Tony indicated an exit at the opposite side.

"What's your etiquette regarding these slaves?"

That information was crucial to avoid making mistakes in

the prestigious club. To think Adrien hadn't known about it until a couple of weeks ago. Someone in another club had mentioned it, and Adrien had wriggled an introduction.

"At nights, they are available to all our members," Tony explained. "They provide all services but are forbidden from leaving their assigned posts." He eyed Adrien before continuing. "If you wish to have a private hour with one or all of them, you can do so during the daytime."

"I see." This policy would certainly cut down the competition. Good thing, he was always free, night or day. "And what happens after the month is up?"

"They'll be part of Club Sortilege's pool of slaves if they so desire." Tony was quick to elaborate. "Anyone can request them for group or private services, and they have the power to accept or decline." He pursed his lips. "Since you're new here, let me tell you that we take our slaves' wishes seriously. We protect them and consider them as human beings first. If they want to play slaves, they are free to do so, but their consent must always be expressed and can be revoked anytime, including during play. Is that understood?"

"Not just understood." Adrien nodded in approval. "It's highly appreciated. What I had expected from such an eminent establishment as yours." He beamed in satisfaction. "I had noticed it upon talking to Miss Yvette Carlisle, who is an exceptional woman."

"She is, isn't she?" Tony seemed momentarily lost in thought.

"She is," Adrien confirmed, looking around to see if he could find her. "I'd like to thank her for last week's conversation. She gave me some excellent advice."

"I'm afraid you'll have to wait a couple of weeks." Tony smiled apologetically. "I sent her to Tokyo on business."

The man trusted her. It was apparent that there must be a lot more going on between these two beyond their respective roles.

"I have no doubt she'll succeed whatever her task." Adrien was sure of it. "She struck me as being highly intelligent and perceptive."

"I wouldn't have assigned her this important transaction otherwise," Tony assented. "Now, if you'll excuse me, I'll see to my other members." With a broad sweep of his hand, he encompassed the entire place. "Make yourself at home and let me know if you have any questions." After bending his head, he spun around and strode toward a nook with two leather couches around a low table.

CHAPTER THIRTY

"What do you think of our latest slave of the month?" Approaching him, Master Devon seemed to be fishing for an invitation to sit down on the couch Adrien had occupied since entering the chamber.

"He looks good enough to eat," Adrien mused, sending the naked redhead another appraising glance.

Back, wrists, and ankles strapped to the X-cross, the young man made an enticing picture, not to mention exciting with his half-mast cock proclaiming to the world what a kick he was getting from the attention and teasing of the masters and mistresses.

"Yeah, doesn't he?" Devon also stared at the bound figure.

"Would you like to sit down?" Switching his focus on Master Devon, he gestured at the empty seat next to his.

"Thanks," the man accepted promptly.

"Can I offer you a drink?" Spotting the lounge's waiter, Adrien signaled to him.

"I'll have a Scotch," Devon told the waiter.

"A Negroni for me," Adrien requested. He addressed Devon as soon as the waiter had gone. "I'm glad this one made it through Presentation Night."

"The best ones usually do." The man smiled broadly.

"I suppose you're speaking from experience," Adrien inquired.

"Yes, I've been here quite a while," Devon confirmed. "I can safely say this is one of the best clubs in all of New Orleans."

"So, they tell me." Adrien was quick to confirm. "That's why I joined."

"You won't regret it." Devon's gaze cut to the cross on the wall.

A mistress was pawing the redhead's penis. Twisting and gliding, she didn't stop until it had become quite a visible erection. She called another slave and ordered her to suck it.

The only catch — he wasn't to come.

Adrien followed the action with a great deal of interest.

Something in that redhead called to him, and he'd hoped that by merely being able to watch him, he'd manage to determine what was so special about him.

"Mistress Fanny will give him a hard time." Devon grinned. "She's a sucker for pretty boys."

The young man was obviously feeling the strain. His dick had become double its original size and was in danger of exploding anytime soon.

"The poor guy isn't going to last very long," Adrien observed.

At that moment, Fanny blocked the female head bobbing up and down that splendid shaft.

The waiter bringing over their drinks distracted his attention so that the cock was standing down when he looked again.

"She must have a lot of experience with them." The Negroni was cold and bitter, exactly how he liked it.

"She has." Devon took a long swig from his drink. "She's trained quite a few of them. Only, she's too demanding to settle on one alone."

"She hasn't claimed ownership to anyone here?" To be honest, most slaves he'd seen had no collars save for Yvette.

"Most of the masters here have no privileged sub." Devon set the record straight. "What about you?"

"Nah, I don't have one, either," Adrien admitted.

Mistress Fanny had allowed the female slave to continue pampering the redhead's dick while a burly master had clamped his nipples. Now, he tortured those same pinched buds by pulling on the chain that connected the two clamps.

Caught between pain and pleasure, the young man seemed to be enjoying himself immensely, at least judging from his cock that was rigid once more.

"I'm not against it." Adrien returned his focus on Devon. "I just haven't yet found one that worked for me."

"That's my problem, too," Devon confessed. "In general, it's not easy to find someone who fits all your needs to a T."

"Who'll keep the same level of high excitement throughout the ownership," Adrien declared. "In my experience, slaves usually perform less if they know they're part of an exclusive agreement. If instead, they have no certainty, they'll give it their best effort every time."

"How true." Devon nodded in agreement. "I never thought of it that way, but it explains why my second time with the same slave is never as good as the first."

The action over at the redhead's side was becoming steamier by the minute.

Evidently fed up with the cross, the burly master had freed him and had him kneeling in front of it. Two bodyguards were tying the wrists of his back stretched arms to shackles hanging from the wall.

The position looked most uncomfortable, though it was just the start.

After fitting a blindfold on the striking hazel eyes, the bodyguard applied an open-mouth-gag and snapped up his head.

"Well, Master Rochefort is going for the serious stuff." Devon chuckled, clearly following everything happening at the other end of the chamber.

"He'll have no trouble getting it." Adrien joined in the

amusement.

The way they had propped up the redhead, it was doubtful he could refuse anything.

Sipping his Negroni, he watched Master Rochefort's not-so-limp piece slide down the redhead's throat.

The young man sputtered a few times, but all in all, he didn't cringe or pull away. More than that, he surged forward every time the master shoved, plainly relishing the dick aiming for his belly despite all the obstacles standing in its way.

Gripping the man's head between his palms, the master fucked his face to a frenzy until he got lost in the rhythm and the depth.

This slave was simply too arousing, and his eagerness got the master undone.

As predicted, Master Rochefort didn't last long. With one forceful blow, he stuck the whole of his engorged rod to the root and unloaded.

"That slave isn't half-bad," was Devon's conclusion.

"Not at all." Adrien had to suppress the impulse to get up and stick his half-mast dick down that inviting gag. "Maybe, someone will claim him before the month is over."

"Slaves of the month can't be claimed," Devon rebutted. "Not until their month is up." He took another sip of his Scotch. "These slaves are a bit different from the regular ones. Their consent is given for granted because it's the primary condition to become a slave of the month. That's why they can't refuse anyone requesting their services and have to submit to all of the club's patrons."

"He's certainly worth trying." His shaft's decisive tug agreed with his assessment wholeheartedly.

"Yeah." Setting his drink aside, Devon settled more comfortably on the couch. "But I'd ask for a private sitting to see if his performance is as good as it looks. I have the feeling this slave gets off from the attention of an audience and might be disappointing in private."

"I'm not so sure." His attention on Devon alone, he ignored Mistress Fanny as she glided a massive plug inside the redhead's derriere. "Why don't we try him together?"

"You mean the three of us?" In spite of his earlier statement, Devon's interest was piqued.

"No, I mean the three slaves of the month and the two of us." He had no problem spelling out what he was already picturing in his head. "Of course, we'll make this pretty redhead service everyone as a way of a lesson, so we'll see how good his performance really is."

"Sounds good." Devon glanced at the bright orange plug sticking out of the gaping ass. "Shall we say tomorrow morning?"

"That'll be perfect," Adrien acquiesced, enjoying how deeply Mistress Fanny was impaling the plug.

Devon scoffed. "Though I fear he'll be a disappointment."

Adrien didn't think so. Quite the contrary. He had the feeling the young man would prove to be incredible on a one-to-one basis, and he couldn't wait for the next day to test his hypothesis.

Chapter Thirty-One

"Good morning, Master Ascott." Opening Club Sortilege's front door, a petite blonde bowed to him. "I'm Lidia Ravel, the club's manager." She gestured for Adrien to come inside. "How may I help you?"

"The Grand Master isn't here?" Stepping in the large foyer, he noticed that the place looked different in the mornings, and not just because there was a frenzy of cleaning going on.

"No, he usually isn't at this hour." Following his gaze, Lidia fixed it on the servants dusting the big pictures hanging on the wall while others polished the marble floor further away. "I'm authorized to assist you in the same way he would."

Meaning, she was the Grand Master's vice.

"All right, then." Adrien had to look down to catch her gaze. "I'd like to see the slaves of the month in a private room."

"Very well, Master." Lidia nodded. "Which ones would you like?"

"All three," he was quick to provide. "Master Devon will be joining me."

"Okay." She sounded as though she approved his choice. "I'll have one of the servants escort you to the private room." Turning, she called out, "Tom, come here."

A young man approached. "Yes, ma'am?"

"Please take Master Ascott to the blue private room." She indicated the door on the far end.

"The one we just finished cleaning?" Tom wanted to be

sure.

"Yes, that's the one," Lidia confirmed before switching her focus on Adrien. "If you follow Tom, we'll send the three slaves right in."

"Thank you, Mistress." He bowed.

"No, no mistress." As red as a tomato, the woman looked adorable. "I'm simply a manager, nothing else."

"Forgive me." Grabbing her hand, he brought it to his lips. "It was a mere compliment."

"I . . . I . . ." Stammering, Lidia flashed huge blue eyes on him. "Thank you."

Looking nervous, she gave him the impression she'd snatch her hand away, so he released it.

"Please, follow Tom," she repeated, clearly glad she had her hand back.

"All right." Adrien stepped behind the young man. "Don't forget to send Master Devon in as soon as he arrives."

"Will do." Lidia disappeared inside the main chamber.

After going through a couple of hallways, Tom ushered him inside a cozy room with a fireplace, a bed, a sofa, a table, the usual BDSM gear, and two crosses. The appellative of blue came from the color of the carpet and walls, a deep blue that would've soothed the most agitated persons.

As soon as Tom retreated, Adrien inspected the props available.

Dildos and plugs of all colors and sizes were lined up in neat rows. On the wall, whips, paddles, and crops hung from pegs. There was also lube aplenty, ball gags, blindfolds, handcuffs, chains, and just about anything one could desire, including condoms.

That every member was required a thorough check-up with relative bloodwork every six months was a strict rule that allowed to dispense with the inconvenience of those rubber caps. They could be used anyway as part of a scene, beyond their sanitary purpose, so every club provided them in abundance.

"Here they are, Master." Hearing Tom's voice behind him, Adrien spun around and saw them.

The slaves were crawling on all fours, as was customary. Stopping in the middle of the room, they pressed their foreheads to the carpet, assuming the submissive position.

They all looked good, but his dick tightened at the sight of the redhead. Definitely, there was more to this young man than met the eye.

"Thanks, Tom. You can go."

Having dismissed the man, Adrien waited for him to leave before he whirled back to the tools he'd been examining. Ignoring the trio, he continued perusing the offering as though he'd never seen anything like it before. Selecting a whip, he tried it out, satisfied with the crackling sound it made. He also chose a sizeable plug, colored bright orange, and a big black dildo that looked formidable. Taking his time, he looked over everything else until he'd pretty much memorized what was available.

Only then did he turn to glance at the three prone forms.

None of them had moved, which was the testimony of good training. Evidently, Club Sortilege took discipline seriously, and he couldn't be more pleased.

Truth was—he wanted to test their limits and break them.

CHAPTER THIRTY-TWO

"Sorry I'm late." After walking through the threshold, Devon closed the door behind him. "Ah, they look quite obedient and docile."

"Just these two." Fending the whip, Adrien struck the two female slaves. "This other one, instead." He hit the redhead in the derriere. "He doesn't seem good enough for anything."

There, he'd set the mood of their scene.

"I agree." Picking up his thread, Devon moved to the props table, grabbed a paddle, then thwacked the redhead on the same buttock. "I don't know why they bothered choosing this one." *Whack, whack, whack.* "He seems worthless."

Going for utter humiliation was undoubtedly bound to raise everyone's level of excitement. Adrien already spotted the tell-tale signs on the women, so moist their cunts gleamed. He and Devon were also nursing the start of a sizeable erection. The redhead was the hardest to read since his prone body hid his dick's reactions.

If he was a slave worth his name, he was getting a kick out of it, too.

"They might have pitied him." Several lashes landed on the redhead's exposed backside.

"A mistake we won't repeat." A few more hearty blows, then Devon dropped his paddle. "'Cause we've got something much better here to serve us." Yanking up the brunette's hair, he smashed her face against his crotch.

"Couldn't have said it better myself." Throwing away the whip, Adrien clutched the other woman.

She was blonde, less curvy than the brunette, slimmer and leaner. Not exactly his type, but he'd make her do.

"His only use is to service these sluts." For good measure, Devon slapped the brunette's generous breasts while directing his engorged equipment down her throat.

Since this was the lowest form of servitude, it was like inflicting a double penalty on the redhead.

"Mine needs a good-sized plug in the ass," Adrien remarked, catching sight of the blonde's tiny butt. "*Now!*"

It was an order pure and simple, one the young man scrambled to obey.

Crawling on all fours, he went to the table and retrieved the orange plug.

Retracing his steps, he stopped in front of Adrien and held it up.

"Impale her ass," Adrien commanded without looking twice at him.

His act was all pretense. He was studying the young man and would've much preferred playing with him. The redhead also seemed to respond to Adrien's interest. His fat cock at half-mast testified to that.

"Hurry." Adrien's voice hardened. "I haven't got all day."

Hastily, the redhead scurried to the blonde's derriere.

"First lick her ass," Devon was quick to block him while fucking the brunette's face. "Or you'll never get that plug inside."

Yeah, a dry fit would probably spoil her pleasure, and consequently, his own.

The young man didn't wait for further instructions. Face buried in the slave's ass crack, he pampered the tantalizing curve with a great show of tongue and fingers, the last an initiative no one had sanctioned.

"No fingers." Interrupting his deep-throat blow job, Devon bent to retrieve the paddle and connected it to the redhead's butt. "I just told you to lick."

Dropping his arms to the side, the young man quickly adjusted his service.

Now, all Adrien could see were the gusty laps swamping the blonde's ass, something the woman obviously enjoyed a lot.

"Enough!" He raised his voice, "Plug her now."

At the sight of the big plug being screwed up that small ass, his piece jerked. It made quite a picture!

As soon as the redhead had accomplished his task, Devon barked, "Now, bring me a dildo for my slut." Without further delays, he resumed feeding the brunette his quite gigantic beast, forcing it down to the balls.

On his part, Adrien picked up the petite blonde and carried her to the sofa.

Flat on her back, he spread her legs.

Not enough. He had to fit an open-mouth-gag if he wanted her to be as defenseless as possible. It took only a few minutes. Then, she was ready for him.

On the other side of the room, the redhead had taken Devon a huge black dildo and was pushing it into the brunette's cunt from behind, doggy-style.

On glimpsing the twitch in Devon's shaft, he knew the game was getting the better of him. Of Adrien, too, considering how eager he was to stick his rod inside the insignificant blonde.

"Ah, one final rule for everyone." Rounding the side of the couch, he went to stand above the blonde's mouth. "Slaves aren't allowed to come unless we say so."

It was usually the most inhuman of orders a master could impart. The most delicious, too, because it inevitably spiraled play to an uncontrollable high.

"Excellent thinking." Devon immediately approved. "Let's see if they'll stick to it." Dragging the brunette to the couch, he placed her in front of the blonde's splayed legs. "Your job now is to lick her pussy."

Oh, my, could anything be crueler?

Bending, Adrien penetrated to the root in the blonde's gaping mouth at the same time that the brunette's tongue brushed the bare and silky slit.

He had no trouble seeing how puffed-up the woman's clit was, ready to explode if the brunette kept up her steady pampering. Just for the fun of it, he made it more difficult for her by stroking it and trying to catch the slithering tongue every time it landed on his fingers.

Devon was focusing on his pleasure instead. He'd raised the woman's hips to his convenience and was about to plunge in her ass.

Deeply embedded in the blonde's throat, Adrien watched the second-by-second action in front of him, from the tip of the erection nailing the puckered opening to the thrust that flung it open. Just like that. One moment, Devon was nudging her narrow entrance. The other, he was up to her guts.

Adrien's cock yelped from the need to come.

It was all too exciting, mainly since he had his eyes on the brunette's sinewy curves. The black dildo stuffing her pussy and the sexy swell of her double bellies hanging added to her allure, making him wish he was ramming her behind instead of Devon.

To stifle the impulse to exchange places, he yelled at the young man, "Lick this other slave's cunt."

It wasn't fair that only the blonde should suffer, right?

It was apparent that Devon was on board with this new command. His cock tripled in size and slammed in what had once been a narrow hole with an upbeat that was sure to crack it sooner rather than later.

Adrien also increased his tempo in the wide-open mouth. Without any annoying teeth to contend with, the gag was easing the sperm's rise to the tip of his bulging crown. A couple of more slides and he'd have no choice except unload.

Devon was close to a spill, too. His frantic blowing of the big butt he'd possessed so masterfully was a sure indication the end was near.

As was Adrien's.

When Devon pulled out and started spraying the brunette's back with fat drops, Adrien didn't linger. Jerking his dick out of the blonde's mouth, he shot semen all over her breasts and belly.

Best of all, none of the three slaves had come and were still hard at work on their assigned tasks.

CHAPTER THIRTY-THREE

"I want her ass." Adrien indicated the brunette as soon as his cock had stopped flooding.

"Be my guest." Devon bowed slightly. "I wanted to try this other one, anyway." Going to the blonde, he pulled her up as he sat on the couch. "You, bring me another dildo," he growled at the redhead.

Settling on the plush leather seat and placing the woman on the floor, between his legs, Devon removed her gag and pressed her face on his crotch. "Suck, slut."

Adrien strapped the brunette on the bondage bench.

Back stretched out on the hard surface, legs and arms splayed, wrists tied, she made a pretty picture.

His dick didn't need sucking. It had become as rigid as a pole the moment he'd touched her. Without further ado, he unscrewed the dildo from her front and shoved it in her ass.

Not as easy as it sounded. The dildo wasn't precisely shaped for the backside. Lucky, though, her gaping ass was nice and large from the earlier fucking. A few pushes and the tip of the giant toy slid inside.

A muffled moan escaped the brunette's lips. Uncaring, Adrien kept shoving until he was sure it wouldn't fall out in the middle of the action. Then, he impaled her pussy and was soon lost in utter bliss.

The dildo was doing a fantastic job of cramping her backside, so her cunt was tighter than ever. Like a heated sheath, it fit his entire girth like a glove, and there was no describing the sheer pleasure of it all.

On the opposite side, the young man had fetched another colossal dildo for Devon, whose piece was now as thick as it had been before his orgasm. Clutching the blonde from under her armpits, he lifted her in the air effortlessly. She was so petite that she hardly weighed at all.

"Free her ass," he croaked to the young man, who quickly unplugged her.

Making her straddle him, Devon directed his hungry monster inside her ass. A relatively easy take, considering how large her butt already was.

Adrien followed the beefy equipment impaling the blonde to her guts. So high up, she sat on Devon's crotch. Taking advantage of their position, the man pushed her toward the floor. Exposing her gleaming cunt, he stuck the dildo into the hilt.

Adrien had no problems imagining how tight his fit had suddenly become, which sparked the need for a change in his arrangement. Not that he'd grown tired of the brunette's pussy.

Far from it.

Change was the essence of erotic interplay. He emptied all her holes and proceeded to stuff them back again, plug in her slit, dick in her rear. The new combination was also delicious.

He had the full cramped effect of her behind, further increased by the toy occupying her front space. Drowning, he set on a steady rhythm that was meant to blow her ass to bits. Kind of like what Devon was doing to the blonde, splitting her ass in two while driving the dildo with such force, Adrien expected it to come out of her mouth.

Exceptional, if it weren't so exciting, which required another adjustment on his part. Switching between the brunette's front and backside, he sank his stiff monster in her cunt again, fitting the dildo through her puckered entrance.

The change was sublime, and he pumped strenuously to

reach her belly. Perhaps, if he went fast enough, his balls would slip inside as well. Just wishful thinking, of course. Still, his beast accelerated at the mere thought. The most thrilling part, though, was noticing how close to a come both women were.

His brunette was barely holding it together. The woman's slit was a dense ocean of honeydew, and her clit throbbed furiously. On the other side, the blonde also gave off signs of an impending climax. Which one would first break under pressure?

Devon turned the blonde around.

No longer facing him, she still sat on his crotch, the marble-like piece firmly stuck in her behind. In this new position, Devon could use the dildo in her pussy more effectively, ramming it in and out to imitate a double penetration.

Watching it from a distance, Adrien knew he couldn't hang on for much longer. That toy moving at the same tempo of Devon's hips was making minced meat of the blonde's pussy while the dick in her derriere was cracking her ass. When she gasped in pleasure, everything happened at once.

The brunette came and the waves cramping her flesh made Adrien unload before he had the chance to pull out, the same way Devon was doing in the blonde's capacious butt.

CHAPTER THIRTY-FOUR

"Well, well, someone is in dire need of punishment." Hardly recovered from his tremendous come, Adrien pulled out of the brunette's snug confinement.

"Definitely." Unscrewing, Devon also seemed ready for business. "You," he yelled at the redhead. "Get up and tie these sluts up to the cross."

Good thing there were two X-crosses available.

The young man executed the order without delay. On his feet, he speedily bound the first one, then the other. Ankles and wrists secured, faces pressed to the cross, they presented their exposed backside.

Devon and Adrien took turns with those naughty derrieres of theirs. Using paddles, whips, and crops, they struck the meaty buns until they were black and blue.

Well, not quite. Still, both slaves were a great deal redder than when they started.

The two women put on a brave face up to the tenth strike. Then, they couldn't hold it together, and their growing pain was made more evident by their attempts at an impossible escape.

"I think they learned their lesson." Folding the whip, Adrien studied Devon's face.

"Have they?" The man delivered another couple of blows before inspecting his handwork. "I think they should be kept here for at least another couple of hours to meditate on how little slave-like they have behaved."

Maybe a bit excessive, but Adrien could understand.

Their disobedience had been without precedents. Only a severe punishment could compensate.

"Very well." After shifting his focus, Adrien's gaze fell on the redhead, and he couldn't help the jerk in his dick at the sight of how aroused the slave was.

The young man's cock was practically giving a standing ovation to the severe disciplining. All at once, Adrien wanted nothing more than to remain alone with him.

"Let's call the manager and tell her right away," he suggested.

"Here." Going to a bell rope hanging on a side, Devon pulled it.

Both he and Adrien were dressed and presentable by the time a soft knock interrupted them.

"Come in," Devon raised his voice.

Lidia's beautiful face appeared at the door. "You called, Masters?"

"Yes." Devon stepped forward. "These two slaves have disobeyed our direct order not to come."

By Lidia's drawn face, Adrien guessed this indeed had been a terrible breach in etiquette.

"They'll have to be kept bound and tied to the cross for at least two more hours." Devon moved toward the threshold.

"I see." Lidia stepped aside to give him room to pass.

"Master Ascott." Whirling around, Devon stared at him. "It has been a most productive morning. Thank you." He bent his head. "I hope we can arrange for another satisfying scene soon."

"I'm sure we will." Adrien also bowed as a way of showing his respect.

"Milady," Devon addressed Lidia. "Thank you."

"Thank you, Master Devon." Lidia pursed her lips. "And you, Master Ascott." Her gaze switched to Adrien. "For taking care of the discipline of these unworthy slaves."

"My pleasure," Devon replied.

Then, he stepped into the hallway and was gone.

"My pleasure, too." Adrien grinned at Lidia.

She was remarkable, even if she wasn't anything like the type he usually preferred.

He would've also wanted to deepen this acquaintance, had not a more pressing need diverted his attention on someone else entirely.

"Will you also be leaving?" Lidia's big blue eyes locked on him.

"I'd like a few hours alone with this other slave." He pointed at the redhead. "It also would be splendid if I could have a bite to eat."

With all the hefty fees he paid to be a member, he hoped it wouldn't be out of the question.

"Certainly," Lidia agreed immediately. "I can arrange another private room and will send Tom along with lunch." She paused to catch her breath. "Would that be acceptable?"

Chapter Thirty-five

It was more than acceptable.
It was perfect.

He had the redhead all to himself with lunch as a bonus. What more could he require?

As soon as Lidia had taken him into the new room and left, Adrien asked the first thing that was on the tip of his tongue. "What's your name?"

The young man's lovely, oval-shaped, hazel eyes widened as though Adrien had committed a capital offense.

"You can answer," Adrien was quick to reassure him. "It's not against the rules to know a slave's name." At least, he hoped not.

"My name is Lucas," the redhead provided.

"Lucas what?" No, a simple name wouldn't do.

"Lucas Dubois." He bowed exaggeratedly. "At your service."

"You can say that again." Adrien chuckled, thinking about what services to demand.

A knock reminded him of how empty his stomach had become.

"Come in," he yelled in the direction of the door.

Tom walked in with a full tray. "Here's your lunch." Striding to the table, he set it down. "Enjoy." A glance Adrien's way and he was out of the room.

"Are you hungry, Lucas?" From the brief survey of the food Tom had brought in, Adrien already knew it would be too much for him.

Again, the young man regarded him with stupor stamped all over his beautiful face. "Me, sir?"

"Yes, you." Nearing the table, he settled on a chair and gestured toward another. "Come on." He patted the seat persuasively. "I'm not going to bite." He chuckled. "And there's way too much food here for one person alone."

"If you say so." Not really convinced, Lucas dragged himself forward on all fours.

"You can stand," Adrien objected. "What do you say if we suspend the rules for the duration of this lunch?"

"If you want, sir." However little he showed it, this proposition was definitely to Lucas's liking.

On his feet, his tantalizing naked body displayed in all its magnificence. He quickly crossed the room and sat next to him.

"Good." Adrien beamed at him, hoping to put the young man at ease. "Now, let's see what the cat brought in."

While looking over the tray, his taste buds watered at the sight of the shrimp cocktail, the tomato consommé, three fillets of sole meunière, a large salad, and a generous serving of potatoes. A bottle of French rosé had been left at the center of the table.

"Wine?" Picking it up, he read the label. "It's a twenty nineteen Château des Bertrands Rosé from Côtes de Provence." As expected, the best rosé came from his native land. "It's excellent."

He knew it for a fact, even if he hadn't yet tasted this particular brand. Then again, he was a connoisseur, and wine was one of the few pleasures he hadn't outlived yet.

"Sure." From the casual way Lucas held up his glass, Adrien judged that the young man knew nothing of wine.

After filling two glasses, he raised his own and touched its rim against Lucas's. "To us," he toasted.

With a flowery bouquet, the sip he savored had a

wonderful flavor and went down silky and smooth, reminding him of the refreshing river water he used to drink when young.

"Excellent." His tongue cliqued against his palate. "What do you think?"

"It's good." Noncommittally, Lucas set his glass back on the table.

"Tell me the truth." Surveying the food, he spooned the consommé into two bowls and handed one to Lucas. "Have you ever tasted wine before?"

Taking the bowl, Lucas became as red as the soup he was about to eat. "No, sir," he confessed at last.

"I thought so." His first spoonful of consommé tasted divine. "Well, we can certainly work on it."

"Yes, sir." Lucas wolfed down the soup as though he were starving.

He was very lean, as a matter of fact. Maybe, food deprivation was another part of Club Sortilege's training.

"Did you like it?" Adrien took his time to finish his practically full bowl.

"Delicious!" Lucas smacked his lips, his gaze falling on the other plates.

"Go ahead." Adrien invited him to proceed. "Help yourself to anything you like."

"Thank you, sir." Grabbing a dish from the stack of empty ones, the young man piled it high with everything available.

"Boy, you must be hungry." The plate looked so full Adrien feared it would spill over in a matter of seconds. "Don't they feed you here?"

"They do, but . . ." A deep blush spread on his lovely face. "I'm always hungry."

From the thinness of his body, Adrien supposed the man hadn't had it easy.

"How old are you, Lucas?" After the tomato consommé

was gone, he took a long sip of wine before taking a generous serving of shrimp cocktail, one of his favorite dishes.

"Twenty-one, sir." Lucas was devouring the second plate, too.

"How's your life been so far?" Rough, if he had to guess. Something about this young man appealed to his instinct of protection, an instinct he hadn't known to possess until he'd seen Lucas.

"Not a happy one," the redhead confirmed, refusing to meet his gaze.

"Tell me about it." Adrien prompted gently, interested in hearing his tale.

"There's not much to tell." Lucas shrugged. "I'm a product of the foster-care system." He seemed absorbed by the sole he was gulping down in large chunks, but it was just a show. "My mom, she put me up for adoption as soon as I was born."

"You never knew her," Adrien interjected.

"No," Lucas was quick to point out. "Even if I had the chance, I wouldn't have particularly cared to."

There was an understandable bitter edge in these words.

"She left me to fend for myself." Lucas moved to the potatoes. "That's what I did for all my life." He ate a forkful of salad. "No one adopted me. I just went from one home to the next until I was sixteen years old."

"I take it foster-care wasn't all that great." Playing it like he was only making small talk, Adrien avoided looking the man's way, focusing all his attention on the dwindling shrimp cocktail.

"Foster-care was sometimes good, sometimes not." Lucas stopped eating altogether. "Sometimes, it was a nightmare."

The hair raised at the back of Adrien's neck in warning. Had the boy been abused?

"You don't have to go on if you don't want." Setting down his fork, he locked his gaze on him.

"No, I . . . I . . ." He took a deep breath. "I want to." However hard it was proving to be, he didn't lower his gaze. "Forgive my presumption, Master, but ever since I laid eyes on you, I felt that we were . . ." He hesitated a moment before he evidently made up his mind and whispered, "Hem . . . connected somehow."

Funny, Adrien had grappled with the same sensation without being able to give it a name.

"I don't mean any disrespect," Lucas hastened to add.

"None taken." Adrien smiled confidently, though he kept up his guard.

No use giving too much away until he knew for sure where this conversation was leading.

"Is that your coded way of saying you think I might understand?" Adrien teased to set him at ease.

"Yes, exactly." After regaining his confidence, Lucas's beautiful face split in a wide grin.

"What did you mean about the foster-care being a nightmare?" Adrien prompted.

"That those foster parents weren't always nice." A scowl crossed Lucas's face. "That some of them liked pretty boys a bit too much."

The picture in Adrien's head was becoming sharper by the minute. "Is that how you had your first sexual lessons?"

No use beating around the bush. Better to spell it out and get it out in the open.

"You could say that." Lucas's expression brightened. "They started me very young."

"You must've hated it." Adrien pursed his lips.

"At first, I did," the redhead confirmed. "Until I found it was an easy way to make some extra money."

"Hush money." That wasn't hard to figure out at all.

"You could call it that." Lucas smirked conspiratorially. "Let's say my foster mothers didn't always know what my foster fathers were doing to me."

"I'm sorry," Adrien wanted to say, yet something in Lucas's dignified demeanor prevented him. It appeared the man had made his peace with his past, however terrible it sounded, and Adrien didn't want him to feel pitied or, worse, patronized.

"I see." Averting his gaze, Adrien kept busy with filling his plate with what was left of the sole meunière. "I'm going out on a limb here and venture that this skill came in handy when your foster time was over."

"How did you know, sir?" Frankly astonished, Lucas regarded him with awe and wonder.

"Just an educated guess," Adrien lied, unwilling to let him know how much this tale pained him.

True, abuse and prostitution often went hand in hand, but it wasn't fair all the same.

"Well, Mister Educated, you're right," Lucas joked. "I kind of lived in the streets for most of my adult life, selling off what I could of my body."

"No drugs?" Adrien inquired.

"Nah, not my thing." The redhead waved a dismissive hand in the air. "I never tried them, never wanted to have anything to do with them." He sounded too firm and sure of himself to leave margins for doubt.

"Good." Polishing off his sole, Adrien tried a few potatoes. "When did you discover your propensity for slavery?"

The question was a formality. Given the young man's experiences, he had no trouble figuring out where and how this particular propensity had developed.

"I suppose all those foster fathers influenced me more than I care to admit." Lucas exhibited no qualms in admitting it. "I've always liked older men ever since I can recall."

Again, no surprise. It was what the absence of a father could do to you.

"Then, I must be a disappointment," Adrien mused. "I'm not much older than yourself."

"Are you, sir?" Lucas's penetrating hazel gaze narrowed on him. "It's funny, but you feel like someone much older." Switching his focus, he stared at an invisible point in midair, seemingly lost in himself. "Like someone who's lived for ages." Then, he shook himself free of whatever had taken possession of him. "Sorry, sir, I didn't mean to offend you." His lips curved downward. "It's just that you feel awfully familiar to me, and I know that even if you're young, it's like you've lived for a lifetime already."

The man was plain amazing!

How he could've picked up on something like that was beyond Adrien.

"Today, when you were disciplining those other two slaves, I noticed how much more master-like you were compared to Master Devon," Lucas continued. "Not that he isn't a master worth his name." He corrected himself hurriedly, realizing his blunder. "You seemed less angry and, therefore, more in control."

The man was not stupid, either, Adrien was happy to note.

"Did you wish you were in the women's place?" Clearing the table of the empty dishes, Adrien leaned forward. "Did you wish I was whipping you instead of them?"

"I . . ." Again, an adorable blush spread on his face. "I . . ." He drained his glass of wine to divert his focus. "I suppose I did," he blurted out eventually.

Adrien chortled in triumph. "So, you like pain, don't you?"

CHAPTER THIRTY-SIX

Huge eyes fixed on Adrien, Lucas simply nodded. "What if I handcuffed you now and cracked your ass without any preparation?" Yanking his thick, short, red hair, Adrien forced him down on his knees. "What if I forbid you to come?" Dragging the man closer, he snapped up his head. "Would you like that?"

"Whatever pleases you, Master." Lucas met his gaze unflinching.

If anything, Adrien was excited. His shaft's sudden jerk was all the indication he needed. "Or maybe, I should go." Playing it like he'd lost interest, he tossed him away and shifted his attention to the wine glass. "Since you're probably not worth my time." Sipping the cold rosé was another way of testing Lucas's reactions.

"No, please, Master." The hazel eyes widened further. "Don't go," he begged. "I'll do anything you demand."

"Anything?" Adrien raised an eyebrow.

"Yes, anything." Lucas nodded earnestly.

Toying with the glass, Adrien wondered why the last thing he wanted to do was take the man in his arms, holding and kissing him until the end of time.

"Let me see your ass before I decide." He made it sound as though it would be a generous concession on his part.

Lucas rushed to comply. Turning around, he pressed his head on the carpet and lifted his hips, the round cheeks in front of Adrien's face. The redhead had a nice backside, no question about it. It was enticing with that sensual and shaven crack dividing the two buns while slanting seductively to the puckered hole.

Adrien's piece stirred in hungry anticipation.

"Have you ever heard of the Marquis de Sade?" Clasping the buttocks firmly, he pushed them further apart.

"Not in detail." Lucas shrugged.

"Then, let me teach you about him." Taking a spoon, he shoved its thick handle inside the man's ass ring.

Lucas cringed and would've dropped to the floor had Adrien not held him by the hips. "Don't you dare move," he hissed. "Didn't you say you were willing to do anything?"

"Yes, Master." Catching his breath, Lucas got a hold of himself.

"This is one of the Marquis's lesson." He rotated the spoon and screwed it deeper inside. "He liked to say, *One must do violence to the object of one's desire. When it surrenders, the pleasure is greater.*"

"Am I the object of your desire?" Lucas's words held a faint sneering trace that was quite inappropriate.

"I don't desire sluts." To reprimand the insolent puppy, he cramped his ass with the addition of the knife's handle. "I'm just taking advantage of what you're offering."

"Is that another of the Marquis's quotes?" The redhead seemed to provoke.

"As a matter of fact, it is." Letting go of the improvised plugs, he stroked the redhead's dick that had become a veritable monster. "It went something like this. *The most fortunate of persons is he who has the most means to satisfy his vagaries.*"

That time, Lucas didn't try to be a smart-ass. His cock stiffening all together kind of kept him distracted.

Adrien slapped him hard. "Hey, remember you're not allowed to come."

"Yes, Master." It was evident it'd be real challenging for any serious compliance.

Having every intention of denying him until the end,

Adrien retrieved a crop from the props table and struck him a few times.

The beating had the opposite effect of what he wanted. Instead of softening Lucas's cock, it grew to a marble-like consistency. The man would've done great in the Marquis de Sade's time. Removing the cutlery from his ass, Adrien replaced them with a giant dildo that he worked inside and out to enlarge the ring to his satisfaction.

Lucas was barely holding on when he was flattened to the wall.

With a few quick gestures, Adrien shackled his wrists, then pushed a bench forward and straddled it, his colossal beast aimed right at the buns. Next, he freed the puckered entrance.

"Now, you'll have to do all the work, my boy." Wrenching Lucas's hips, he brought them down on his equipment and centered the delicious ass ring. He flung it wide-open from the forceful impact and didn't allow it to get anywhere but over his erection in spite of the man's attempts at taking it slower.

Instead, Adrien's monster penetrated to the hilt in one blissful shove.

Lucas groaned.

"That's right." As a way of an incentive, he circled the slave's waist, grabbed his pole, and jerked it seductively. "Your job now is to get my cock to your throat." Letting go of the delightful rigidity, he slapped the buttocks pressing on his crotch. "So, get a move!"

Weighing on his arms, Lucas lifted his ass, threw it back down, then raised it again to repeat the sequence. It was the beginning of a fantastic rhythm that would soon blow that magnificent derriere to bits, aside from draining the man's energy. With all that up and down movement, his arms would become as inflated as those of a weightlifter.

Adrien's only contribution to the exhausting effort was to

push up his hips to increase the redhead's slam-down effect. For everything else, he was getting lost inside the heated sheath swallowing him whole, balls excluded, unfortunately. Rather than being admitted inside, they slapped Lucas's thighs with a clap that became louder the more frenzied the dance.

He would've unloaded right there and then had something not alerted him that his slave was about to be very, very disobedient.

"Remember, there's no coming for you!" His sharp command threw Lucas off.

"Master . . ." Out of breath from his exertions, he sounded at the end of his wits. "I wasn't — "

"Save it," Adrien snapped, accelerating his upward swings. "Let me come in peace."

That the young man gritted his teeth at the news was evident from the loud huff escaping his lips, not that Adrien gave a fig about it.

The tip of his bulging crown was about to explode from the slave's latest throwback. He gripped Lucas's hips and slammed them down hard, then held them as his fathead burst.

Literally.

An explosion he hadn't been ready for shot his semen to the man's guts.

Literally.

CHAPTER THIRTY-SEVEN

"That wasn't so bad." Toning down his enthusiasm, Adrien let go of Lucas. "Wouldn't you agree?" Getting to his feet, he untied the man, who would've dropped to the floor had he not held him.

"Yes, Master." Of course, it was a lie.

Then again, how could Lucas be truthful when his whole body screamed for the denied release?

"Is that so?" Dragging him, Adrien sprawled him on the bench he'd just occupied. "Then, why is your cock so hard?"

Naturally, it was a trick question. There was no right answer, and the redhead realized it immediately. "I . . . I . . ." He blushed violently. "I'm sorry, Master."

"I didn't ask if you were sorry." Clutching the taut penis, Adrien jerked it, which started a renewed erection for him. He usually had a brief recovery period. Probably all the years of fucking had something to do with it, but this seemed too much. Boy, would he ever get enough of this tasty slave?

"I asked why your cock is so hard."

Continuing the sensual slides would only lead him into trouble. Lucas, too, considering how beastly his shaft was turning out to be.

"Could it be because you want to come?" Adrien playing cat and mouse was sure to accelerate both their demise.

Lucas gulped. He was trapped, and he knew it.

"Well?" Adrien gave the rod a stronger tug.

"Yes, Master." Evidently, having found his courage, Lucas raised his voice a notch, "I would."

"Would you now?"

The man's cock so appealed to him Adrien did the unthinkable. He swallowed it. Bending on the fat crown, he drew it all inside his mouth. It was extraordinary!

Strange yet true, he loved it, the feel as much as the taste of that firm, solid male equipment.

Lapping it vigorously, Adrien sucked it almost to the balls. When he returned up, he caught Lucas's gaze. "Don't you dare come," he warned.

"No, no, sir." The poor fellow was barely holding on, which only added to Adrien's fun.

Licking and rubbing the long length didn't improve matters for poor Lucas. His cock kept growing until Adrien feared he would explode. Since he couldn't delay the inevitable, he switched to serious action.

His own piece had become monstrous anyway, so he might as well stick it where it belonged.

In Lucas's gaping ass.

One thrust and Adrien was up to the hilt. From there, he set an energetic tempo that was sure to bring both of them over the edge. Only thing, the redhead needed more instructions. Leaning on him, Adrien trapped the man's equipment between their bellies. "Now, you can come for me."

Then, stretching further, he did something even more unimaginable. He kissed Lucas.

No, devoured his lips would be more appropriate. Attacking his mouth, he stuck his tongue down to his throat. Sweeping it as though it belonged to him, which oddly, it did. For the moment Lucas sucked him, awareness hit him like a blow to the stomach.

Julia Le Clerque exploded in his consciousness.

Oh, crap.

Julia Le Clerque was the reason behind his longevity, the endless and repeating cycle of his life, and the energy-sucking business. She was the reason behind his fucking deadly karma. Like Yvette Carlisle had guessed, Julia had cursed him!

As his brain raced through his last conversation with her, he recalled how desperate and hopeless she'd been and how much she'd insisted on that soul mate stuff.

He had scorned it, denied it, and still had a world of reservations about it.

Yet, it was the key to it all, and that was a mere starter. Unbelievable yet true, Lucas was Julia reborn.

As impossible as it seemed, this man was the reincarnation of his dead mistress. Intensifying the kiss, Adrien wondered whether the extreme pleasure of it all was going to his head, or maybe, he was going mad.

Either way, the conviction that he'd suddenly found what he'd been looking for so long persisted, growing stronger the more he fucked and kissed this amazing man.

Deep in Lucas's mouth and ass, Adrien began to lose all perspective. All boundaries, too. He didn't know where he ended and Lucas began. Then, Lucas climaxed. So hard, the ripples of his peak crushed Adrien's dick. The next thing he knew, the vortex blew him away. With a gasp, he flooded the capacious butt holding him prisoner while his tongue still ravaged the moist cavity above.

When the seizures of orgasmic pleasure abated, Adrien tossed back his head. At a loss for words for the first time in his life, he wondered what to tell this young man. That he was his soul mate? That he'd been searching for him for one hundred thirty years? That he was Julia Le Clerque, come alive again after he'd pushed her to suicide? That he wanted to spend the rest of his life with him, however long it would turn out to be?

All these questions and more crowded his mind, but how to utter them without sounding like a ranting lunatic?

"It was about time!" Lucas's clear, high-pitched voice scattered all his nonsensical thoughts. "What took you so long?"

EPILOGUE

"Well, well, look at you two." Yvette Carlisle approached Adrien's booth. "I hear congratulations are in order."

"They are." He squeezed Lucas, who was sitting opposite him in Club Sortilege's plush lounge. Then, his gaze switched on Yvette. "Will you join us for a drink?"

"I'd be happy to." She slid in next to Lucas. "When's the happy day?"

"Tonight," Adrien announced.

It was Halloween, after all. Not simply his birthday, but also the end of a one-hundred-thirty-year-old curse. How could he be sure? Wasn't it obvious?

He didn't feel any weakness, didn't feel the slightest bit depleted of energy, had already fucked Lucas's brains out, and the man wasn't dead or anything.

No, he was sitting right here after Adrien had kept him in bed for the entire day.

Ah, what a relief!

It was goodbye negative karma, hello positive karma.

In other words, goodbye death, hello life.

Yvette turned to the redhead. "Aren't you excited?"

"No." The oval-shaped hazel eyes were all on him. "I'm damn ecstatic!" His focus swung back to the woman. "But also apprehensive."

"That's the spirit," she confirmed. "Collaring is a serious step in our lifestyle and should never be taken lightly on either side."

Spotting the waiter close to his booth, Adrien made eye

contact.

"What would you like, sir?" Approaching, the young man eyeballed him alone.

"Miss Carlisle, what will you have?" Adrien beamed at her. "A Long Island Iced Tea?"

"Please, call me Yvette." She returned his smile. "And yes, I'd love an Iced Tea."

"You, Lucas?"

Adrien still couldn't believe it.

He was here with the man, and they'd been together for the past seven months, practically inseparable.

"I'll have a glass of champagne." Lucas's gaze lingered on him, evidently asking for his approval.

"Great choice." Adrien grinned encouragingly.

His training of Lucas wasn't limited to sex. He'd broadened it to include lessons in etiquette, gastronomy, and enology.

"We'll have a champagne bottle and the Long Island Iced Tea," he told the waiter.

"If you don't mind, Master Ascott, I'd like to drink the champagne with you." Yvette objected.

"Fine, we'll take a bottle of rosé champagne," Adrien addressed the waiter. "Do you have Devaux des Bar?"

"No, sir." The man shifted on his feet. "We have the twenty eighteen Veuve Clicquot La Grande Dame Brut, two thousand six Dom Pérignon Brut."

"No, they're overrated and not worth their absurd price." Adrien scoffed. "Anything else?"

"Let me see." Frowning, the waiter counted on his fingers as though he was making a list of his stock, "We also have Dosnon Brut Côte des Bars —"

"That's best served with a meat dish," Adrien protested. "What about the Besserat Cuvée des Moines Brut?"

The waiter's expression brightened altogether. "Yes, we've

got that."

"Great." Adrien waited until the man had left before his gaze returned to Yvette. "Have you ever tasted rosé champagne?"

She shook her head. "No, Master Ascott—"

"Please, call me Adrien." He interrupted her.

"All right, Adrien." She said it like she was trying the sound of it. "I have a confession to make." She leaned forward gingerly as if she was about to reveal a long-buried secret. "I've never tasted champagne, rosé or otherwise." She looked at Lucas. "What about you?"

"I tasted it only once." Straightening, his gaze turned to Adrien. "The regular kind, not the rosé." Then, he glanced at her. "Master Ascott is teaching me all about wines."

"He seems well-learned," she agreed and added mischievously, "And not just about wine."

"He certainly is." Lucas's face colored red. "I realized how much I didn't know simply being with him these past months."

"How long since you guys found one another?" Yvette's perfectly shaped eyebrow rose.

The waiter bringing Besserat with three glasses interrupted the conversation.

Adrien himself opened the bottle and poured the bubbly ruby liquid, the notes of dark red coming from the berries. He handed the glasses around before raising his. "To you, Yvette."

"To me?" Surprise lit her lovely green eyes. "Why?"

"You made me see things in a different light." Adrien sipped the cold champagne. "You told me gender shouldn't be an issue when you're looking for someone." The taste was just right, and it slipped down his throat refreshingly. "Remember our conversation here?"

"Of course." Yvette also drank champagne. "Aha! That's

how you found one another."

Adrien appreciated her discretion. Another woman wouldn't have wasted a second to blurt all that soul mate nonsense, which wasn't nonsense at all.

The months he'd spent with Lucas were all the proof he needed.

Grabbing his lover's hand, he smiled. "Let's say there's a connection between us."

"That goes beyond our present relationship." Lucas ended his thought.

That settled it. When Lucas had come out with that absurd question, Adrien hadn't known why it had taken him so long to figure out things. Why it had taken him one hundred and thirty years to realize that Julia had been lying in wait all this time. She was the reason he hadn't aged a day past twenty-one, the reason he still walked the Earth while all his nearest and dearest were long gone, the reason he hadn't been able to build any meaningful relationship. My God, he must've been blind, deaf, and mute to miss what had been in front of him, what had been staring him in the face ever since her suicide.

Worse, he had allowed it to go on for as long as it had, callously unconcerned if he sacrificed an innocent life every Halloween.

Yes, that had been the price of his thick-headedness, of his failure to comprehend. The price she'd charged for what he'd done to her and her family. His curse also for being so insensitive and arrogant to believe that revenge was a one-way street.

Now, he knew better.

If Julia's death had fulfilled what the Marquis de Sade had said a lifetime ago, "*My vengeance needs blood,*" Adrien's lonesome yet deadly longevity had been Julia's payback. Singlehandedly, she'd condemned him to become a killer, to live alone, and miserable for eternity. What better way to exact her retribution?

One life against hundreds, he knew the balance had been all in Julia's favor, and she hadn't relented until it had dawned on him what she'd wanted him to understand.

"Other people might say we are soul mates," he continued dryly. "Julia certainly would have." He paused. "Do you remember her?"

"I do. She was the one with the bad mojo vibe." Yvette laughed, taking another sip of champagne. "The one who believed in romantic love, soul mates, and all that jazz while you despise all of it," she was quick to recall.

"I still do." Savoring the rosé's strong flavor was a real pleasure. "But I can't deny the connection between Lucas and me." Again, he couldn't tear his gaze away from the hazel-eyed one. "That goes beyond any love or sex." He took a deep breath. "What's important is sharing your life with someone." Yeah, it was what Julia had wanted him to understand. "Because without sharing, there's no growth."

He could more than testify to that, he who had remained unchanged for the past one hundred and thirty years. Finding Lucas had saved him from repeating his mistake over and over again. Recognizing Lucas had broken his deadly karma. Most remarkable of all, once he'd come full circle, his biological clock had started ticking again, which was the best news of all.

"Is that what Lucas taught you?" From her concentrated expression, it was clear Yvette was taking his words very seriously.

"No, that was Julia's lesson." Adrien set the record straight once and for all. "Lucas only reminded me of it."

"Then, tonight, your ceremony is more than a regular collaring."

Somehow, the woman connected the dots all too easily.

"Right." Lucas's bashful smile was adorable. "We've got a

lot to celebrate." He fingered a slim gold collar Adrien had given him that morning and that he'd immediately worn regardless of the fact the event had yet to take place.

To think that Julia would've been a perfect sub had he not treated her as awfully as he had.

"Tonight is the beginning of the rest of my life," Adrien observed.

"Of the rest of our lives," Lucas corrected immediately.

"Exactly." He clasped Lucas's hand more tightly. "The beginning of our lives."

"I'll drink to that." Yvette toasted them with her raised glass. Then, she took a generous swallow. "I'm really happy for you." She drained the glass. "But now, I've gotta go, or the Grand Master will have a fit." She giggled as she got to her feet. "I promised to help him set up things for tonight's festivities and the Halloween party that will follow, and I'm already late." Smiling brightly, she was about to walk away but stopped at the last minute. "Oh, Adrien, one last thing and forgive me if I bring this up." Her startling green eyes narrowed on him. "I hope I'm not offending you, but you look so much older like you've aged a lifetime since I last saw you." She studied his face intently. "Are you sure everything is fine?"

"Everything is just perfect." And it was about time.

At last!

Don't miss more Halloween books by Laura Tolomei

Bondage Slave for Hire

Nothing satisfies Lilly. Not even working at The Dungeon BDSM Club as a bondage slave for hire, a slave looking for her true master. None have fit the bill so far. Until Terry. He spins her craving to fever pitch, and she might just fall in love with him if she could only be his slave. Not just that master's. His own, too, his gorgeous Creole lovers. They are the perfect Masters, but also keepers of the Black Room. On Halloween, she'll discover just how bad and dangerous their pain-lust game can really be. Will she be able to fulfill their true needs? Or will she perish in the attempt?

Novel—BDSM, Gay LGBT, Ménage à trois/quatre, Multiple Partners, Paranormal, Horror, Shape-shifter

The Demon Waiter

He hadn't expected it, not at all. And yet, there it was, Laurent De Berger's heart wish was . . . impossible! To think he'd done it by the book, had sex in a dusty ghost town saloon with Anthony and Renée on Halloween night, only to find out–no, he still couldn't believe it! But, since there was no going around it, what to do now?

Novel—Gay LGBT, Ménage à trois, Dark Fantasy,

Paranormal, Horror, Shape-shifter, Romance

Bloody Passion

There's a hidden treasure inside everyone. Some show it, but only a few can afford it. Sometimes, you only need to know how to manage the other's treasures, even if self-destructive. In the end, it's like seeing yourself in a mirror. So how to explain the violence?

Novel — Gay LGBT, Ménage à Trois, Dark Fantasy, Paranormal, Horror, Shape-shifter

Visionquest

It wasn't till he took me to his bed and made love to me, for the first time. No competition between us, no unspoken challenge, no master-slave, no blood, no death, nothing but intense emotions overwhelming me with the sheer power of his feelings, a sea so deep, a tide so strong I thought I'd drown as he took me face up, raising my legs above his shoulders and plunging deep before preying on my mouth, too, in a never-ending kiss that took my breath, not to mention my resolve, away — that in spite of everything, I gave him what he wanted most, my soul in its entirety, for I knew right there and then I was sealing my destiny forever.

Novel — Gay LGBT, Ménage à Trois/Quatre, Dark Fantasy, Paranormal, Horror, Shape-shifter, Romance

Sacrificial Sex

An all-powerful sorcerer rules a primitive world of Aztec-like pyramids and bloody rituals that apparently appease sanguinary gods when in fact satisfy a deep-rooted bloodlust and sexual craving on innocent virgins. A young man from another more, advanced world, tries to stop the carnage. An intended victim himself, blood and sex are the only weapons at his disposal. The task is far more than expected, and he will get more blood, sex, and lies than he ever bargained for when his technological future impacts this primordial past.

Novel — Gay LGBT, Ménage à Trois, Dark Fantasy, Sci-Fi, Paranormal, Horror

About the Author

Born in Italy, Laura Tolomei lives in Alicante, Spain, and is the author of thirty plus books in her very particular and unique genre—Erotic Romance with an Edge. She has been traveling the globe since age five and has no intention of quitting. After having been an avid reader her entire life, she decided at age forty to write her own stories and has not looked back since. Writing novels that are on the boundary of accepted conventions—erotic romances with an edge—is her trademark, and she guarantees an erotic earthquake with each book. Among others, they include the scorching dark fantasy *Virtus Saga* books, all eight of them, along with the kindred spirits of both the *ReScue* and the *Soulmate* Series, not to mention her horror novels along with a few historical ones.

For more info, check out Laura's website:
www.lallagatta.com
www.lauratolomei.com

www.ingramcontent.com/pod-product-compliance
Lightning Source LLC
Chambersburg PA
CBHW060811120626
46557CB00001B/167